Time Changes Yesterday

Nyengi Koin

Copyright © Nyengi Koin 2024
All rights reserved.

This book is copyright material and must not be copied, reproduced, transferred, distributed, licensed or publicly performed or used in any way except as specifically permitted in writing by the publishers, as allowed under the terms and conditions under which it was purchased or as strictly permitted by applicable copyright law.

Any unauthorized distribution or use of this text may be a direct infringement of the author's rights and those responsible may be liable in law accordingly.

ISBN: 978-1-957076-33-1

Contents

Chapter 1 1

Chapter 2 11

Chapter 3 23

Chapter 4 37

Chapter 5 47

Chapter 6 65

Chapter 7 79

Chapter 8 87

Chapter 9 107

Chapter 10 123

Chapter 11 135

Chapter 12 147

Chapter 1

Enitan Browne brought out a simplified edition of Oliver Twist and started reading the atmosphere her class-mates had created around the room. She had read this particular edition about three times already, but right now she had nothing to do. How she wished her daddy would let her stay at home sometimes and not come to school, until they had a new teacher.

Like everyone else in Primary 5A, she loved being able to do whatever she liked most of the time without the supervision of a teacher, but she was bored stiff at being whisked from one class to the other for lessons. For two weeks now, they had had no teacher. They had to be divided into four groups of seven to be able to take lessons with the other four arms of primary 5 in Santa Maria. It wasn't much fun. The other classes were already full and having seven more children did not help the seating arrangement at all. The hosts felt it was an inconvenience and the guests felt discomfited most of the time. Besides, it was not much fun being with some of the students from these other classes. They were so dull, so scared of the teachers that nothing exciting ever happened there. But primary 5A was different.

Santa Maria was a school where the children were given intelligence tests before being placed into various classes. The set of boys and girls in 5A were a bit more intelligent and developed than most children of their age group. At the ages of ten and eleven, most of them could read and write as ably as a secondary school form 2 pupil. They had all read primary 3 and 4 together.

In fact, with the exception of a few new pupils, they had all been together since Primary 1, Their teachers had always found them a bit of a handful but academically, too good to be true, The noise in the class was getting worse, Enitan closed her book and put her hands over her ears. Just then, Mrs Falolu walked Into Primary 5A with a pretty, elegantly dressed lady, who did not look like any of the teachers.

'Class, this is your new teacher, Miss Odu,' said Mrs Falolu, struggling to be heard above the noise of the students getting settled, and banging their desks. For the first time since the second term started two weeks before, Mrs Falolu, Assistant Headmistress of the Santa Maria Day School, got the full attention of Primary 5A Immediately, The chattering in the class died down; the boys and girls in the back row sat up in their seats. The only sounds were a whisper or two from the back row. Miss Odu was nothing like their last teacher, dowdy Mrs Sawyerr, who had left at the end of last term, because her husband had been transferred to Ibadan and she had had to go with him.

Miss Odu was beautiful and poised, an obvious contrast to Mrs Falolu and the other teachers, with their out-dated clothes. She looked something between twenty five and thirty, but did not try to make herself look older as most of the other young teachers in the school did. She wore a bright green, floral cotton dress and had her permed hair styled beautifully. And on her feet were glamorous, black, high-heeled shoes.

'She is beautiful, abi?' whispered Bunmi, the naughtiest girl in the class to her friend, Enitan.

Enitan, eyes fixed on the new teacher, nodded. There was something about this lady that attracted her. Miss Odu began to speak. I'm pleased to meet you all. I want you to know that I'm always available if you need me for anything other than your studies. This brought some giggling from the back row but she ignored it and continued, 'I want you all to regard me not only as your class teacher, but as your friend too. I'm here to teach you all your subjects. I want to help you with any problems you may have or any questions you want to ask. Perhaps you may want to discuss your choice of Secondary schools, for example.'

It was obvious to all the children, as she talked, that this was a

very frank and understanding person. All the other teachers never seemed to have enough time for the pupils outside classes. In spite of her youth and good looks, she seemed almost motherly, with a confident and sympathetic voice. As the children listened to Miss Odu, Enitan suddenly had a wonderful idea in her mind.

Having never known her own mother, she was always pleased to meet someone who was motherly. For a year and a half now, she had been trying to find a replacement for her. This annoyed her sixteen year old sister. Joy who wanted no such thing and was always having it out with Enitan, though their father knew nothing of this.

Miss Odu's voice jogged Enitan back into the present. 'I don't want you to hesitate for any reason before coming to me. Don't feel too shy or think your worries are too childish to tell me. This is part of my job. Don't think your problems are too serious for me to tackle. If I can't help you, I'll try to find someone who can."

Elizabeth Kofoworola Odu paused for a moment and glanced around the class, as if to convince them of her sincerity. She felt so nervous in front of all those pairs of small eyes staring at her. There were twenty eight students in the class, and most of them were probably spoiled, pampered little things as was to be expected of this posh school. She felt far from the confident expert she appeared to be. She had been teaching before, but one can't help feeling nervous when taking up a new job, and a class of ten to eleven year olds at that.

At the Holy Child Primary School, she had been teaching a class of seven and eight year olds, and they were all darlings. She felt sad leaving them, but she needed a change and the money that came with this job. 'Any questions?' she asked loudly, trying to look straight at the little faces.

'Yes,' said Kenneth, from the back row, raising up his hand, Miss Odu was to come to know him as the naughtiest boy she had ever taught, and the cleverest. "What's your phone number?'

There was some subdued laughter at this. All the children wondered how Miss Odu was going to react to this unnecessary question.

'There's no need for that. After all, you'll be seeing your teacher in school everyday,' put in Mrs Falolu sharply.

Unruffled, the new teacher turned to Mrs Falolu and said,

'That's all right. He's only a kid.' To the class, she said with the same calmness, 'I'm afraid I'm not on the phone. I'm sure you all know it's only the rich and fairly well to do who own telephones in this country. But I can give you my house address, if you want it. 'Yes!!!' shouted the whole class and Miss Odu rattled off her address; and to the surprise of the children and Mrs Falolu, she even wrote it down on the black-board. The Assistant Headmistress opened her mouth in amazement, then smiled, as the whole class hurriedly wrote the new teacher's address down in their books.

'I think I'll leave you now, Miss Odu, to get to know your class better,' said Mrs Falolu and left the room. Miss Odu then asked the children if they would like to tell her their names starting from the front row. The children got up one by one, and prattled on with bored expressions.

The new teacher did not miss the looks on their small faces, so she said brightly, which was far from how she felt deep inside her, 'I've got a better idea. Let's make a song out of it.' The children stared at her expectantly.

'It's a simple song,' she continued. 'It goes like this.

My name is Kofo, Kofo, Kofo.

My name is Kofo.

And who are you?'

She sang it again pointing to the girl in the first seat, who got up and sang after her. So the children soon got the hang of the song and sang it cheerfully.

In the afternoon, they all filed out of the door to go home.

Enitan Browne packed her books in her bag, and glanced through the pages of her note books, found where she wrote Miss Odu's address, and put it in her bag, feeling quite pleased with herself. Her friend Bunmi, came up behind her and asked, pointing at the notebook, What are you taking that home for? We haven't got any homework.

Enitan sighed impatiently. Sometimes this Bunmi can be so thick. Notebooks mean nothing but homework to her. If you take all your books home, she thinks you don't want to tell her about some assignment she herself hasn't heard about, thought Enitan to herself.

'It's just a notebook.' She smiled at Bunmi.

"I know it is a notebook,' answered Bunmi irritably. 'But why are you taking it home? That's what I want to know. Anyway, you always take your books home.' Enitan smiled. That was one thing about Bunmi she was grateful for at this moment. Bunmi asked a lot of questions and supplied the answers. She did not have to talk much in Bunmi's company, and right now, Enitan's mind was working like a clock, so she did not feel a bit like talking.

As they walked out of the school gates, Bunmi brought out a packet of sweets, popped one into her mouth and started chewing it noisily. She offered Enitan one but Enitan refused and glanced at Bunmi's teeth. And as if reading her friend's thoughts, Bunmi said, 'I know I'm not allowed to eat sweets but I simply crave them. Mummy will kill me if she sees them.' Enitan looked at Bunmi and thought, Lucky you to have a mummy! For the umpteenth time, she wished she had a mummy too. Nobody bothered about her teeth as long as they were clean and did not hurt her. She had no one to talk to about what she felt.

Joy was away at boarding school, and their father, wonderful though he was, did not understand much about childish or girlish things. He worked hard all day at the Electronics Firm where he was Public Relations Officer and came home, looking very tired and worn out every night. He loved telling jokes and reading stories to Enitan and Joy. Every night, he told her what happened at work and she told him about school. His face would light up when you told him jokes, and when you let him tell you. He always bought her and Joy a lot of clothes - nice, expensive clothes. He had very good taste, and where clothes were concerned, one could scarcely know they had no mummy.

Both Joy and Enitan knew that their mummy's death had hit their father pretty hard. She had died a couple of days after Enitan was born, so the little girl had not known her at all. But from the photographs she saw of her, Joy was their mummy all over. And that is probably why daddy loves her so much, Enitan thought quietly to herself. Enitan had practically been brought up by her father's elder sister, auntie Shade. Auntie Shade had five children of her own, three of them older than Enitan. She had had a happy time with them, but it was nothing like having your very own mummy. Sometimes, auntie Shade took sides with her daughter, Toyin, who was about the same age as Enitan, when they quarreled and scolded only Enitan. Then at other times, she remembered that Enitan was motherless and spoiled her, overlooking anything she did.

At five, she had been brought back to daddy's house, to come and live with daddy, Joy and their grandmother. She was very happy because she had wanted to stay with Joy. Joy was always bringing her things when she was at auntie Shade's. They had been very close, and Joy had watched over her like a hen over her chicks those days. Now they were always falling out whenever Joy came home on holidays from school, because she would not stop matchmaking. However, she missed Joy very much when the latter was at school. Joy told her about their mummy, but daddy never talked to Enitan about her and she had asked no questions, because Joy had told her not to. When Bunmi was going into their car, she turned to Enitan and said, "Are you still going home with me or not?"

Enitan shook her head. She really would have loved to go home with Bunmi. There were always lots of things to do at Bunmi's house. All her family, especially her mummy, were very nice to Enitan. She knew Enitan had no mummy, and she allowed them to play all about the house, and told them lots of stories. If she had not been married to Mr. Shode, Enitan would have tried to get. her to their house. But today she had much to do, in the way of plans for getting Miss Odu to come to their house.

I'm sorry, Bunmi. I can't go with you. I've just remembered something my daddy told me to do,' she apologized.

'Are you sure we have no homework?' Bunmi asked, popping another sweet into her mouth. 'I'm sure,' Enitan replied, and said goodbye. She waved at Bunmi's car, took off and hurried home, full of excitement. She could not wait to get home and think of how to get Miss Odu to meet her daddy.

Chapter 2

For quite a long time, Enitan had been trying to find a wife for her daddy, and a mother for Joy and herself. The idea had first occurred to her when Joy was home on holidays. She had been reading a comic in the sitting room, where Joy and two of her friends were talking about boyfriends. Joy had a boyfriend but the other two hadn't and were lamenting over their fate and saying it looked as if they would leave secondary school without having had a boyfriend. Then laughing, Funmilayo Bakare had said, 'It's all right for us. We are still only in form three. But think of all those older people who haven't got any like us. Take my mum. She hasn't got a husband or a boyfriend-nothing!'

'It must be awful for her,' said Ngozi.

'You are telling me!' laughed Funmilayo, and they all laughed.

They thought it was a huge joke.

Enitan did not feel it was funny at all. She felt very sorry for poor Mrs Bakare. She was sure Mrs Bakare was as lonely as poor daddy. That was when the whole thing first struck her. She could not wait for Joy's friends to go. She felt sure Funmilayo would be good as a sister. She had lots of clothes and was very popular with Joy's other friends at school.

She was a day student, but every visiting day, when Enitan went with daddy to see Joy, she was always around, joking with other girls. They all called her 'Barkis' and had lots of fun with her. Enitan felt sure her mother must be just as pretty and as popular as Funmilayo, and what she wanted in a mother. When both girls went home, Enitan spoke to Joy. 'Joy,' she said, 'why don't you invite Funmilayo's mummy here?'

"What for?' asked Joy, surprised.

"Well, you know, just for her and daddy to get to know each other.'

'And what do they want to get to know each other for?' asked

Joy sweetly, raising her eyebrows.

Enitan felt uneasy. She knew this sweetness meant that Joy did not approve. She knew Joy did not understand, and she was finding it difficult to put her plans into words. Joy could be very tough if she did not like or approve of something, but she was always good to Enitan. She loved Enitan very much, and put up with a lot of things from her that she would never take from anybody else.

Enitan shifted her weight from one foot to the other and said,

'You know Funmilayo's mummy hasn't got a husband, and daddy hasn't got a wife. I thought it would be nice if they could get married to each other.'

'I see,' Joy laughed. Enitan smiled. She thought Joy liked the idea and was glad about it. 'It would be nice to have Funmilayo as a sister, Enitan went on excitedly.

'No, it wouldn't,' said her sister firmly, pulling her onto the settee. 'She's all right as a friend, but as a sister, no thank you, Enitan. You better get that idea out of your head. You don't know that our daddy or Funmi's mummy would like it. Daddy, for one, won't thank you for it, so forget it.'

Joy got up and went to their bedroom, and Enitan knew better than to follow her there and start discussing the topic again. She knew that she had been dismissed, but she could not get the idea out of her mind. She wondered why Joy was not keen on it. It seemed an excellent enough idea to Enitan's small mind. She kept scheming and plotting and finally decided on what to do.

The next time Funmilayo came to their house, Enitan spoke to her while Joy was in the bathroom, taking her bath.

Funmilayo,' she began shyly. 'You know the last time you came here, I heard you saying your mummy hasn't got a boyfriend. Our daddy might like her and they might get married. Funmilayo laughed until her sides ached. "You are a funny kid, Enitan,' she laughed.

'I'm serious,' said Enitan.

Funmilayo thought this would be a very good joke. She was a practical joker, always ready for any sort of dare and would do anything for a laugh. She looked around her thoughtfully at the Brownes' beautifully decorated sitting room. There was a four chair suite, very elegant wall cabinets, a heavy sound system, colour telly and lots of decorations. She decided she would give it a try since Mr. Browne was rich. She knew her mother would come anyway, as long as there was money involved. She loved going out with rich men and having a nice time.

'All right, Enitan. Would your daddy take my mummy to a nice place?' she asked. 'Oh yes,' replied Enitan confidently. 'Anywhere she wants to go. Will you bring her here?' 'Yes,' said Funmilayo. 'Your daddy wouldn't agree to come to our house, would he?'

'No, he wouldn't,' said Enitan. She paused, and thought for a moment before adding, 'But please don't tell Joy. She doesn't want to hear of it.'

'All right then,' smiled Funmilayo. 'When shall I bring her?' Enitan thought for a while and then said, 'Why don't you bring her on Saturday evening? Joy's going to a party then.' They agreed on after six on Saturday evening, and both kept it a secret from Joy.

On Saturday, Funmilayo and her mummy arrived a few minutes after Joy left. Joy had taken a longer time than usual to dress up for the party. 'Goodness, I'll be late!' she exclaimed, looking at the clock. Do take me in the car, daddy, please!' 'Oh no!' Enitan could not help a loud protest. 'I'll be here all alone at home,' she added weakly, seeing their surprise. 'Anyway, the place is just around the corner. Why can't Joy walk there?' Joy looked at her thoughtfully.

'Well, Enitan, if you don't want to be left here alone, you can come with us,' their father suggested. 'I'm tired.' Enitan sounded peevish. 'I don't want to go out.' 'Look, you've been excited and nervous all day. What's wrong?' asked Joy. Nothing! Nothing's wrong! I'm all right! Really, I am!'

All right. I believe you. Nothing's wrong,' but her father looked a bit worried. 'You don't mind, do you, Joy? I think I ought to stay in with her.'

Enitan knew that if her father took Joy to the party, he might miss the Bakares, or he might go out from there and not return until very late. As soon as Joy left, she said, 'Ah, Funmilayo, that's Joy's friend, told Joy she would be coming this evening. I suppose Joy has forgotten.'

"What a pity,' said their father.

'The least you can do now, daddy, is to stay and talk to her,' suggested Enitan. So he stayed, and they chatted until the visitors arrived.

Enitan jumped up and opened the door, as soon as she heard their knock. She was surprised when she saw Mrs Bakare. The latter was far from what she had expected. She was as fat as a hippopotamus, matronly and far from beautiful. She wore a lot of make-up and a very tight dress. She was nothing like the lonely, beautiful woman Enitan had been expecting.

looked better in Iro and Buba or 'up and down', but in this dress, she looked like 'Mama Saro' or a 'Cash Madam' and Enitan was disappointed. She, however, had to make all the introductions.

'Daddy,' she said unenthusiastically, 'this is Joy's friend, Funmilayo, and this is her mother, Mrs Bakare.' Mr. Browne shook hands with Mrs Bakare and served them drinks. He told them Joy had gone to a party. It was soon quite clear to both Enitan and Funmilayo that their parents had nothing in common, and it had not been a good idea to get them together at all.

Tayo Browne was the only one who did not realize what was going on. He talked and laughed a lot with Mrs Bakare, told them a few jokes and teased Funmilayo about her boyfriends at school. When they finally left, Enitan was quite exhausted and very glad to see them go. She made up her mind not to be discouraged by this little experience. It taught her only to be more careful. Their father told Joy the next morning, at breakfast, about the visit. Enitan concentrated on her food and kept silent. She could feel Joy's eyes on her. When their father left the table, Joy asked her how that happened. She told Joy everything and Joy laughed, until tears fell out of her eyes, down her cheeks.

"Why don't you mind your business, Enitan? If daddy wants a wife, he'll get one himself. And I'm glad you've seen Funmi's mummy for yourself now. Don't do it again or I'll tell daddy, ' she scolded her little sister. I'm sorry,' Enitan said and Joy had said she was going to tell Funmilayo off.

Funmilayo apologized, and said it was only a joke to humor little Enitan.

They would have made a big thing out of it, but Funmilayo was one of those jolly people who could never keep malice, and they had settled it.

Enitan had not been put off by this experience. She only became more careful, never using Joy's classmates, or letting her know. And most of all, she made sure she knew what to expect in advance.

It was not long before the next opportunity knocked at her door.

It was a new neighbour, Mrs Pedro, who moved into the new house in the street, two houses away from them. It was a Saturday, and in the afternoon, Enitan went to see her. Mrs Pedro was a little surprised to see her. Enitan shyly said, 'I only came to tell you that,

I hope you'll like it here, and to see if you had any children I could play with.'

Mrs Pedro smiled, took the little girl's hand and said, 'What a nice little girl you are. Come in. I'm afraid my children are away at school?' She gave Enitan some biscuits and chinchin. Enitan asked her about her husband and Mrs Pedro told her he died over five years ago.

'Oh, my mummy is dead too. She died when I was born,' said Enitan quickly. She looked carefully at Mrs Pedro and thought she was beautiful, and had a pleasant nature. She was a lot better than Mrs Bakare. She looked around her and said carefully, 'This is a big flat for you, when your children are away. You must be very lonely. But then, my dad and I live with my elder sister Joy, and our maid, at No. 23. And Joy is away at school now too.'

Mrs Pedro smiled and said, 'Is that so?' She went on smiling and Enitan was not sure if she was interested or not. She took another quick look at Mrs Pedro's kind face and went on, 'He's very lonely, sad most of the time.' Then she added in a whisper, 'I think he wants a new wife.' Mrs Pedro laughed out loud and tickled the little girl on the chin before saying, 'That's serious!' She had a twinkle in her eyes and looked so amused that Enitan was convinced she thought it was a huge joke.'You don't believe me,' she said. 'I'll bring him here and you'll see.'

'Well, don't tell him I'm in on his secret,' smiled Mrs Pedro.

Enitan thanked her for the biscuits and told her she would bring her daddy over to say thank you soon. Mrs Pedro laughed and thought what a funny girl that was. That evening, Enitan told her father about Mrs Pedro and how beautiful and lonely she was. Then she told him about the biscuits and asked him to come along and thank her.

She kept asking him until he agreed to go. Enitan suggested that it would be nice if they gave her a present. They had nothing, so they had taken her some oranges for a welcome present. Mrs Pedro was surprised to see them, but grateful for the oranges. They talked for about an hour, Tayo Browne telling her where to shop, what plumber to call and to call on him, if ever she needed him for any odd job. Enitan was happy they had so much to say to each other.

She thought it would work out fine. The next day, she was going to Sunday school, when she saw Mrs Pedro, going to church too.

She said good morning and they went on together.

How old do you think your father is?' asked Mrs Pedro, sweetly and suddenly. Enitan was surprised by the question. 'He is thirty four, Ma.

Why do you ask?' she said.

'Do you know how old I am?' Mrs Pedro asked Enitan.

Enitan shook her head.

' Well, I'm forty-eight and I have five children, all older than you, two of them married. I thought it might help you to know that,' she told Enitan kindly with a smile.

Enitan could not believe her ears. Forty eight! That was old.

Mrs Pedro was fourteen years older than her father. She did not want her father to marry a person so much older. If two of her children were married, she would probably be a grandmother by now.

'Yes, thank you, Ma,' she said at last, and was quiet, until she turned the corner to the church.

Then Enitan tried another woman, who lived in the next house.

She was separated from her husband and had a little boy of about ten years old. Enitan did not like the boy. He was too rough, but the boy's mother was not as old as Mrs Pedro, and more attractive than Mrs. Bakare. Enitan told her that her daddy had lots of money but was very lonely and would love to get married again.

She invited him to her house. This time, Enitan did not go with him, but when he came back, it was evident that he had enjoyed the food more than the company. Enitan later found out that the woman had lots of male friends and was always out. She did not want such a wife for her daddy or that sort of mummy for

Joy and herself. She was glad her father did not see her and her horrible son again.

That was over a year ago. Now she was almost ten, and she was sure Miss Odu was the positive answer to her dreams. She would not dream of telling Joy or anybody about her plans, but,

'Please, God, let it be all right this time!' she prayed. Her father would get old without getting married again and that would be awful. She made lots of plans and decided that she would wait for some time before starting on the real match-making. She expected Joy would be mad at her, but who was going to tell her?

Tomorrow she must get to know Miss Odu more, but tomorrow was another day. Today, she must get home quickly.

She rushed into the house and shouted, 'Risi, I'm home!'

Chapter 3

Elizabeth Kofoworola Odu woke up and remembered what date it was. Today was a very special day. It was the seventh anniversary of Bobo's death. The sun was already streaming in through the curtains, heralding the start of another year without him. It was the sort of morning when Bobo would have said, 'Let's go to Bar-beach or Tarkwa Bay, Kofo.' Bobo had loved the beach so much.

He was always so full of life, and they had done a lot of carefree and silly things in those few sweet months, when nobody guessed how short their time together was to be. She had enjoyed those months. Life is so cruel. One day, you can be so fulfilled, the world so rich and full of promise; the next day, it can all be snatched away from you-everything that matters-everything you hold dear.

Kofo, that's what Bobo had loved calling her. Nearly all her friends called her Lizzy as she had gone to a Catholic School, but very soon after she met Bobo, she had asked them to call her Kofo too. She had met Bobo at a friend's party. She was naturally quiet and rather shy. She did not attend too many parties as a rule, but this had been a fellow teacher's engagement party and she had felt it necessary to go. She still lived at home with her parents and they had urged and talked her into going. She was an only child and both parents doted on her.

Bobo had asked her for a dance and she had agreed. But she had not felt in the least interested in him because she had just quarreled with a boy she had been befriending for a long time. They had quarreled because she would not she would not let him go all the way. She was annoyed, not only because he had let her down but also with herself, for she felt a sort of relief at their parting. It was quite clear to her now that she had nor loved him as she thought she did after all.

From the time Bobo had asked her for that first dance, he would not leave her side. He wanted to know everything about her -the kind of childhood she'd had as an only child, the kind of music she liked, her hobbies and plans for the future. Now if anybody else had been so inquisitive, she would probably have been annoyed and told him off. But she was so fascinated by his cheerfulness and good humour that she had nor minded until after the second dance.

He made her laugh a lot, and she was sorry when the long record ended. After the second dance however, she refused to say any more about herself and told him to talk about himself instead. He was just an ordinary guy, a student at the University of Lagos, he said. Then he told her about his two brothers and two sisters and his parents. By the end of the party, he had won Kofo's heart. He asked her if he could take her home and she said yes. But then when she saw his Suzuki, she refused to ride the pillion. It was one of those things she was terribly scared of.

He said he could not bring a car because his father needed it to go out with that evening, and talked her into trusting him on the motorbike. Thinking about it now and remembering the countless times she rode the pillion in the next months, Kofo smiled to herself.

She saw a lot of Bobo after that. He passed his finals and started working with one of the big Engineering Companies in Lagos. When he was alone on his machine, he went as fast as if he was on a race track, but whenever she was with him, he reduced his speed. He got a car very soon and she was happy, because she hated the motorcycle and had feared it too much to feel completely safe on it.

Bobo was tall and handsome and he was always laughing and carefree. That was what had attracted Kofo to him at the beginning, but later it became her main cause of concern about him at the beginning. When they got to know each other more, she talked to him incessantly about his carefree attitude to life. He would only laugh, pull her into his arms, and start singing. Life is too short girl, that's why I must be moving on along?'

He had this idea that life must be enjoyed to the full, while one was alive, or the gates of Heaven would be closed on one. Once he asked her, 'Why don't people face up to the fact that they will die one day? It does not make it easier to bear if one tries to ignore it.'

Bobo was twenty-four and she was twenty, when they first met.

She knew that the whole of his family did not approve of her, because she was Ijebu, but for Bobo's sake, they all tried to like and accept her. His sister, Molara, was the best of all of them. She was next to him in age and loved him very much. She was always very good to Kofo, and she and Bobo between them laughed at their mother's fears of Ijebu people making too much medicine.

When Bobo had announced that they were getting married, they had all put aside their fears and doubts, and had rallied round to help make it a success. It had been a case of joining them as they could not beat them.

Bobo had been a great one for parties. She remembered once when he was very sick, she had gone to see him in hospital and at the sight of his lean face, she had started crying. Bobo asked her, 'What's wrong?'

She begged him not to leave her as she could not bear it if anything happened to him. She could not go on living if he died, she had sobbed.

Bobo was silent for a few minutes. Kofo looked up at him. His eyes were full of tears. It was the first, last, and only time she even saw him cry. He had held up her chin and had said to her, cleaning her face. 'Kofo, don't ever say such a thing again. I am not going to die but whatever happens to me, you must go on. You must and will live your life to the fullest.'

Then a friend of theirs had invited them to her twenty-first birthday party. Kofo told him nothing about it, but Molara took it upon herself to do so.'That's great!' Bobo said enthusiastically. "Why didn't you tell me?" he asked Kofo.'I was going to tell her we can't come," Kofo replied.

"Why not?" Bobo asked, surprised. Well, you won't be well enough by then. You might still be in hospital for all we know,' she explained.

I know I won't be able to go but you are Kofo, and you will go to that party.'

I couldn't go to parties with you here, Bobo. It wouldn't be fair to you,' she argued.

Bobo took both her hands in his. 'Kofo, listen to me. I want you to go to that party. Sure, I'd like to go with you, but I can't, just as we can't always be together in person always. You can be there for both of us. I'll be very happy here, knowing you are enjoying yourself over there, and I'll be looking forward to you telling me all about it. Do you understand me, Kofo?'

Kofo nodded and he continued. 'You know that green dress?

Put it on. I shall be proud to think of you wearing that?' The green dress had been his present to her when he received his first salary. He had been passing in front of this boutique, seen this dress and fallen in love with it; so he had gone in and bought it for her. He had been right when he said he knew the dress would suit Kofo, because it really did. It accentuated all the curves in her body as if it was tailor-made especially for her. So she had gone to the party in the green dress and enjoyed herself.

Bobo came out of hospital and life continued the same. He was back to his old self again and life became another whirlwind of parties and picnics for both of them. They would go to work in the day and meet in the evenings, but during the week-ends, they were always together either in Kofo's parents' house or at a friend's.

It was Bobo who had taught her to swim in the first few weeks after his discharge from hospital. Once when they had gone on a picnic to Tarkwa Bay, she hid in a corner, tired out after all the running and dancing. She stretched luxuriously on a deck chair. In exactly three months time, she and Bobo would be getting married and life seemed promising all round. She was on holiday and had plenty of leisure time to enjoy Bobo company.

Her blissful musings were broken into suddenly, by a violent, "Get up, lazy old cow!' from behind. She turned round and smiled at the young man peering down at her through the rocks behind her. I thought you were going to have a race with me! he exclaimed, as he threw himself down on the deck chair next to her.

'I meant to, Bobo, but I've had too much excitement today and I'm worn out. It was heavenly, just lying here and watching you and the others swim yourselves to wrecks, Kofo laughed

'Lazy girl! You will soon grow fat if you get tired easily. I'll give you ten minutes to rest, and then you must join us, Bobo said, gave her a kiss and went to join their other friends. Kofo's eyes dwelt on him with affection and pride, as he ran quickly down the shore. The well worn term of "live wire" could scarcely have been more aptly applied than to this young man, who radiated intense vitality to all who came in contact with him.

He had boundless energy, a great love of life and high spirits.

Kofo had found in him the ideal companion of her youth, and her warm affection for him had strengthened over the months. Bobo also taught her to play tennis. Even though she wasn't much of a player, he always allowed her to partner him. He never allowed any of his friends who were not good players to do so, since he himself was exceptionally good. Whenever they were losing to the other side because of her bad shots, Bobo would grin at her, his teeth flashing white in his brown face, as if telling her not to worry, and she would grin back at him. It was impossible to be ruffled in his company for long.

He always managed to know when she was feeling sore and would promptly do something to cheer her up. Whenever they were in a sort of gathering and were not sitting together, he would look her way from time to time, catch her eye and smile at her. And Kofo would be conscious of a warm glow spreading from her innermost being, telling her of her love for Bobo.

Kofo could never have doubted his love for her. Just before his death, he had taken her to Ibadan to go and see his godmother, a kind, middle-aged widow, who was very fond of him and he of her. She was very pleased with Kofo and had told Kofo that she was the first girl Bobo had ever brought to show her, and she knew they were going to be happy together. Kofo and Bobo had spent a lovely weekend with Mrs Da Silva.

'Bobo is so considerate with you,' Mrs Da Silva had confided in Kofo, the morning before they left Ibadan. 'And he isn't by nature a considerate young man. He is in far too much of a rush. He's extremely kind and will do anything for anyone, but little gestures of thoughtfulness are not in his character. At least I didn't think so, until I saw him with you.'

'I have found him particularly thoughtful and kind,' Kofo said sweetly. You are so quiet, and the two of you would have seemed a bit incompatible to me. But from the moment I saw you together, I knew you were important to him,' Bobo's godmother told Kofo.

'I'm glad he is settling down with someone like you. You are so restful and your serenity will cool him. You will make him happy,' she concluded.

Kofo thanked her and they left Ibadan that evening and Mrs Da Silva, little dreaming it was the last she would see of her lively godson. Then, a week before the wedding, they had a car accident and Bobo died instantly. It had begun like any other ordinary day. They had both gone to work, and met in the evening, sensing nothing of the disaster that hung over them. Bobo drove quite fast, both of them chatting and enjoying the scenery and each other's company. While Bobo carefully followed the twists and turns of the winding road, they tried to decide what to do over the weekend. But events made that decision for them.

To this day Kofo does not know quite what happened. It was always like a nightmare to her whenever she thought about it. She could only picture how there was this big black object looming on top of them. A lorry had turned in front of their car. Bobo tried to swerve but the lorry still drove straight into them. It was horrible. Kofo could remember both of them screaming, and Bobo's body lurching against hers, trying to cover her. Then there was the screeching of wheels, glass shattering, Bobo's screams and her own cries. Then everything went blank.

There was nothing more she remembered. She woke up in a dazed state. She was bewildered and confused, and fell back into a coma. When she did open her eyes again, it took her a few minutes to take it all in. She was in a strange bed, with people rushing around her, then her blurred vision finally gave way and she could focus properly. She was in a hospital ward, and she could see nurses passing by in their starched uniforms. Her memory had deserted her for the moment, and she still could not make sense of it.

The woman in the next bed saw her awake, smiled at her and spoke to her. 'Good thing you are awake at last. We were beginning to get worried,' she smiled.

Kofo did not answer. She was becoming conscious of the awful ache in her head and all over her body. She wondered what had happened to her for a moment and suddenly, she remembered the car crash. She remembered the terror, Bobo's shouts and his body pressed over her, his hands covering her head from the glass.

Panic and desperation hit her, and she started crying. She called out Bobo's name involuntarily. She wanted to see him.

A nurse came and sat by her bedside, wiping her tears and comforting her, telling her not to worry that the doctor would soon be along to see her.

Kofo looked at her and replied, 'I don't want to see a doctor. I want to see Bobo. Is he all right?' she said.

The nurse bit her lip. An anguished look seemed to cross her young face, and she concentrated on looking at Kofo's chart.

Then she got up saying she would get Kofo a drink, as her throat would be parched by now from all those drugs she'd been given.

Kofo watched her go away and knew that something was wrong. She imagined Bobo needing her and made up her mind to get well soon for him, to be able to look after him. It's weird; when something terrible happens, you never allow yourself to think of any other possibilities but the best. Even while you know there is no hope, you keep hoping for the best. Kofo told herself that Bobo was more injured than she was, and so she must be brave for him.

At last, the doctor came in with the nurse. They drew the curtain round and the nurse clasped hold of Kofo's hand. The doctor spoke rapidly but softly. "It was a bad accident. I'm sorry to have to tell you. Both the lorry driver and your fiancé died instantly.'

Kofo stared at him. She was hardly listening as he went on quickly. You must be thankful you are alive yourself. We'll soon have you better. Both your parents are outside waiting to see you?'

'Bobo? Dead? It can't be true!' Kofo screamed and went on screaming hysterically. The nurse gripped her fingers more tightly, the sorrow in her eyes telling Kofo all she needed to know. The doctor was not lying but she did not want to believe it.

She yelled and yelled and screamed and screamed with the nurse trying to comfort her. Eventually, she felt the sharp prick of a needle. She fought against the injection but it was stronger than she was and she fell asleep again.

When she woke, she came face to face with reality. Bobo was dead. She could cry no more. A deep depression engulfed her.

How could the doctor talk of her being thankful to be alive? Her life was nothing without Bobo. She wished the crash had killed nothing with her because her parents and friends could do nothing with her because she would talk to no one.

She performed the necessary duties for the authorities, answering policemen's questions and all that. She was discharged from the hospital after five days. Then it was Bobo's funeral. She insisted on going. She wore a black dress and watched everyone's grief as an outsider. It was as if she was in a trance, as everything went on around her. Then Bobo's coffin was lifted into the hole and she was asked to pour some sand on it. While she was doing this, it suddenly dawned on her that this was the end. She would never see Bobo again, not ever, and she burst into tears, sobbing loudly. Everybody started crying again too. They were all so touched, because after the first day, Kofo had not been able to cry until that moment. She cried throughout that day.

After the funeral, she withdrew from the world into a shell of her own. She relieved her life with Bobo any time she was awake.

His face was constantly before her eyes and she recalled how happy they had been together. It was impossible for her to go on without him. She was given compassionate leave by her employers and she stayed at home. Perhaps it would have helped if she could have talked about her feelings, about the pain and bitterness, but she had never been good at putting her feelings into words, so she could share her grief with no one. Instead, she carried it around with her, locked in her heart. Everybody tried to be helpful but she would not allow them to help her. Her mother, with the best will in the world, was always trampling on her feelings. She was always saying things like 'Time heals all wounds.' But Kofo thought bitterly that it never would. When you have the bottom knocked out of your life, you can't expect the hurt just to disappear, like a little rain cloud, passing across the blue sky. So the shadow would pass, then the sun would come out and everything would be just the same? It was impossible.

Chapter 4

Two months found Kofo still in this state, then she suddenly realised she was pregnant. She did not know what to do. A baby was the last thing she wanted right at the moment, but she could not get rid of it, come what may.

If Bobo had been alive, she would have been so happy and he would have been thrilled too, because he loved children. This was Bobo's everlasting present to her, Bobo's baby, and it was a part of her, growing in her, closer to her than anybody could ever be to her. Her mother was bewildered when she told her about it, because of Kofo's position at school.

Kofo told the Headmistress and they talked it over. This was a permissive society. She felt it would be all right as most parents were not particularly worried about the teachers' private lives. When everybody knew about the baby, they were full of sympathy and tried to help.

But Kofo wanted no help. She just wanted to be alone with her memories of Bobo. The only person whose company she could stand was Molara. Kofo had always liked Molara, partly because she was so much like Bobo, and closer to him than all the other members of his family but mostly because she had been very good to her. She was the closest to him in their large family and yet made the least show of her grief. She managed to remain cheerful and sensible, so did his parents, although a rare jewel had broken from their family crown. They accepted his death with no bitterness.

Once Kofo heard Mrs. Coker telling somebody who had come to sympathize with her. My dear, who are we to complain? You know that old parable about the cut flower? The gardener asked "Who cut this flower?" And the owner of the garden said, "I did. Then the gardener said, "Who am I, my Lord, to question your will? That is just what this is like.

Molara was the one who made the least fuss over her, seeming to accept her lack of emotion. She always talked about Bobo as naturally as if he was still alive.

Kofo insisted on leaving home, as she wanted to be alone. So she moved to a cozy flatlet despite her mother's disapproval. Her mother was always fussing over her, but her father was as marvelous as Molara. They both respected and understood her need not to be fussed over and they always let her do as she liked.

Even if she sat in their company all day without saying a word, they seemed to understand. She was not exactly looking forward to the baby, but she knew she must have it. It gave her no pleasure since Bobo would not be there to share the baby. He had not even known there was a baby on the way. She did not know how she was going to cope with the baby. There were going to be problems, she knew that.

The baby arrived exactly eight months after Bobo died. Everyone came to see her, bringing her fruit and cards and presents for the baby. They all tried to be cheerful and commented on how much the baby— a boy— looked like Bobo. Kofo tried to share in their enthusiasm but she could not.

One day, Mrs Coker came to see her. She leaned over the cot, lifted the baby up and exclaimed, 'He is lovely, just like Bobo was as a baby!' Kofo tried very hard to smile but it seemed she had forgotten how.

Mrs Coker drew up the chair at the foot of the bed and sat down by the side. 'What will you call him?' she asked Kofo. Kofo did not answer. She just stared at the ceiling.

I know it's early yet, but you must have some ideas,' Mrs Coker persisted. 'Of course he is Babatunde to us. That's the name we will give him, but you might have some other names you want him to have. We want to grant you the privilege of giving him his first name. People nowadays give their babies names themselves anyway, not the grandparents.'

Kofo went on staring at the ceiling. She knew Babatunde, a name which literally means 'father has come again' was apt for calling this baby, but she did not care what he was called.

Babatunde is a common name among the Yorubas for boys whose fathers or grandfathers died before they were born. It was believed that it was the dead man making a come-back through that baby—hence 'father has come again.'

Kofo could not think of any name to give her baby. It was thoughtful of the Cokers to give her a chance of giving the baby his first name. A lot of other paternal grandparents would have insisted on the baby's first name being the name they gave him.

But Kofo did not feel any particular joy at having this baby. She felt nothing for him at all. She could feel Mrs Coker's eyes on her, waiting for an answer. Kofo sighed and said, 'I still don't know. I'll have to think about it. I haven't got the faintest idea what to call him.'

Mrs Coker knew that Kofo would not say any more, so she did not press for it. 'Well, it's still early. He is not even eight days old. You'll know what you want by the time he is eight days old,' she said cheerfully.

She stayed on for about thirty minutes, cooing to the baby and chatting to Kofo. Kofo answered all her questions listlessly, without enthusiasm. Nobody who came to see her could get her to talk much. Her mother did not know what to do with her. When she was discharged from the hospital, she insisted on going to stay in her little flat alone with her baby. Her mother thought she was mad. It was not safe at all for her to stay alone, brooding with the baby.

She needed company, help and also time to get her strength back. Mrs Odu thought of all sorts of reasons to have Kofo stay with her, but Kofo was adamant. Mrs Coker too suggested that Kofo should come and stay with them, until the baby was older at least, but Kofo wanted to stay alone. It was only her father and Molara who understood her.

Her father came to take her home from the hospital, and he took her directly to her flat. The whole flat was spick and span and airy. Kofo found her mother had already loaded the kitchen with all sorts of food and provisions. Kofo smiled ruefully to herself.

Her mother was ready to help in any way, though she was disappointed Kofo would not come and stay. Her father, she knew, had talked to her mother and asked her to leave Kofo to lead her life. Despite the misfortune that befell her, she was not a little girl any more. She was a woman, a mother and she would cope.

He asked Kofo, 'How will you manage your money?'

'I'll be alright,' Kofo assured him. 'I have some money saved. That will be enough to keep me until I start working again.'

'All the same, take this.' Her father gave her an envelope with three hundred Naira inside.

'I don't want it. I don't need it, really, Daddy!'

"Won't you accept a present for the baby?"

She had no answer. She took the money and her father went away soon afterwards. When her father left, Kofo had time to think what a different welcome home she would have had if Bobo had been alive. He would have been so thrilled and she would have been too. She would have been very happy, but now she felt indifferent to this tiny mite that she gave birth to.

She, who loved children so much, could feel nothing for her own child. She did not feel as if he had ever been a part of her at all. She felt nothing like his mother. She wished she could feel differently. She put the baby in his neatly-made cot, and went to the kitchen to make herself something to eat. She found some hot boiled rice, stew and yam pepper soup, so she heated the pepper soup and had a nice hot meal.

Her mother had thought of everything, she smiled to herself, and she was glad about it, because she felt so tired. She went to the bedroom to sleep and just then, the baby whimpered. She loved rocking their babies, but she felt no joy in doing so. Oh, what's wrong with me? she thought. Or is this not my baby? Her mother when she heard about this said maybe she would feel differently with time.

Sunbo Odu came every morning and evening to bathe the baby.

She made so much fuss over the baby that it annoyed Kofo. Kofo still felt nothing for him for another three weeks. She always left him in his cot, and the little baby, as if sensing her feelings towards him, was always quiet, sleeping contentedly after each feed. He was such a placid baby, and gave no trouble at all, except when his grandmother was around. He limited his whimperings to the times Mrs Odu was there to see to him and Kofo could not help feeling, somewhat guiltily, that this baby of hers was hard done by.

Then when he was nearly one month old, her mother gave him to her one morning, after dressing him up and he smiled at her. It was the first time he had really given her such a big smile. Just then, he looked so much like Bobo that Kofo's heart warmed towards him. It was as if her heart had been tied with strings which were now loose. She felt love, so much love for the tiny life in her arms. She felt protective and grateful too, all of a sudden.

This child was hers and Bobo's. Through both of them, the Lord had given life to this little one. And even though Bobo was not here, she should be grateful she had this child, a part of him as a permanent reminder of him. With this little child, she would never forget Bobo. He would always be with her.

Kofo hugged the baby tightly to her bosom and started crying, loud heavy sobs. Her mother was surprised. 'Kofo, what's the matter?' she asked in alarm. Nothing mummy. I've just realized what this baby means to me. It's as if the ties binding me to my grief and bitterness have been broken. Kofo smiled at her mother through her tears. Her mother came to her and hugged her. "I'm glad, she simply said. She could not stop the tears trickling down her cheeks as she watched Kofo looking wonderingly at the baby.

Kofo kept on weeping and smiling and kissing and cuddling the baby.

Her mother cleared the bath things away and came back to find her still gazing at him. 'Well now?' she asked.

'Mummy, I'm going to call him Bode. Olabode Coker. Bobo would have liked that. What do you think?'

I'm glad. I like Bode. Bodes are always handsome and it's nice for him to have a name from you at last,' said Mrs Odu happily.

Kofo knew her mother was very happy that she had decided to call him anything at all. Olabode, like Babatunde, was suitable.

Olabode literally means "wealth has come back". It was particularly suitable for this baby who was replacing a loss. Great wealth had left the Coker family in respect of Bobo's death, but that wealth had returned in the form of Bode.

Soon it was time for Kofo to resume working again. She did not know what to do about Bode while she was at work. She knew her mother was ever ready to look after him, but she also knew that Mrs Coker would not mind looking after him too. Mrs Coker hoped to play a greater part in the baby's life, which was natural as she had lost Bobo, but had gained another son in Bode. But Mrs Coker had two other grandchildren, and Mrs Odu had just one-

Bode—and so it would not be fair to cut her out of the baby's life either.

Kofo did not want there to be any unhealthy rivalry between the two sets of grandparents. So she decided on the fairest method she knew.

She would take Bode to her mother's place for a week, and the following week, he would go to Mrs Coker's house, every morning, and in the afternoons, after school, she would take him.

Both mothers' houses were on her way to the school so it was not much trouble. That way neither of the grandmothers got too jealous. Each tried subconsciously to outshine the other, but there was no bitterness. Kofo, however, made sure Bode knew her as his real mother. She spent all the time she could spare, alone with him in their flat. Her life revolved around him, and that was how they had gone for the past six years. It had not been all that easy, but they had managed quite all right, she and Bode.

Chapter 5

Enitan Browne was a very brilliant girl, the most brilliant in her group, in fact, so it was not long before Miss Odu got to know and like her very much. She gave little trouble in school and this pleased the teacher very much.

Primary 5A was the most notorious class in Santa Maria, but Kofo, when she really got to know them, found them very loving, bright and amusing children. She loved the whole lot of them, and they loved her too, because she was always smartly dressed and pretty. She particularly loved Enitan and Kenneth because they were the two most brilliant children in the class, and they got on fine with Bode. But Kenneth was a real live wire. He played pranks and jokes at the expense of most of the children in the Class.

There was a particular day, when Kofo came to school and found the children in her class sitting miserably. She was immediately afraid something terrible had happened, and she asked them what the matter was, the cold hands of fear clutching at her breasts. None of the children answered.

She asked them again, now more afraid than ever, and they all burst into laughter. There was nothing wrong, they laughed. Had she forgotten it was April Ist, the Fools' Day? Kofo was mad, but she managed to control her temper and see the funny side of it, so she did not punish them. Later in the day, Kenneth and his friends played another trick, this time on Mrs Falolu. She had been going to her class when he called out to her.

Excuse me, Ma, your bag is open."Thank you,' said Mrs Falolu and looked at her bag, which was securely closed. Kenneth and the other boys shouted, 'April Fool!!!' and ran away before the Assistant Headmistress could catch them. Much as she loved him, Kofo was fed up with Kenneth by the time she'd been teaching them for two months.

She felt she'd never seen a naughtier boy. Most times, during physical education lessons, he would be trapezing and displaying all sorts of acrobatics, thus attracting the other kids' attention. They would be full of admiration for him and would lose interest in whatever Kofo was telling them. She would caution him but as soon as she turned her back, he would start again.

More than once, he'd made a fool of her, but he was always sorry afterwards, and would apologize and do his best so much to make up for it, that her heart would melt towards him, and she would forgive him. Once she found him staring out of the window while everybody was busy doing their sums. She called his name and he did not answer, so she went to him and shook him. She asked him why he was not doing his sums like everyone else, and he told her he'd finished. She looked in his book, and found that he had, and had got them all right too. So what could she say?

On another occasion, she was reading a passage to them from the Bible, when she heard a suppressed giggle. She looked up, and noticed that the children's gazes were fixed not on her, but all on one small boy. They were watching Kenneth in admiration and awe. He had made a great big bubble-gum balloon, and was blowing it larger and larger until Kofo thought it would cover his face.

'Kenneth, come here at once!' she shouted, feeling more than mad at him. He deftly retracted his bubble-gum balloon into his mouth, without any smears and spat it into his palm before getting up to her, Kofo did not know what sort of punishment to give him. She gave him six strokes of the cane, but he did not shed a single tear. And then she asked him to change places with one of the boys in the front row, so that she could keep an eye on him always, but it did not do much to help. There just was no stopping him.

Apart from a few others like Kenneth, most of the children in Primary 5A were very good. They all, even the naughty ones, made sure that they did their homework before coming to school. They came dressed neatly every day and kept their class clean at all times. Most weeks, they won the school's award for the cleanest class of the week, which was an oil painting of Little Boy Blue.

Another thing they would have won an award for, if awards were given for it, was noise making. They were famous for that throughout the whole school. They were however quick to understand what their teacher taught them and Kofo was pleased.

She had been given this special class to teach, even though sometimes they amazed her with questions she felt were too big for children of their age group.

As soon as they saw Kofo coming into school, they would run to her and take her bag from her, then one or two of them would volunteer to take Bode to his class. Enitan Browne was especially fond of Bode, and for the first two months, she was the one who usually took him to his class for Kofo.

Enitan began her real plotting a couple of months after Miss Odu became her teacher. She did not do her homework. She did this deliberately, to draw Miss Odu's attention to her, knowing perfectly well that Miss Odu was more annoyed with someone who failed to do their homework at all, than with someone who got everything wrong. All the other children in the class did theirs and the books were exchanged among the class, as Kofo wanted them to mark it themselves.

'Enitan, where's yours?' the teacher asked, noticing that Enitan's partner had no book to mark. Enitan got up and said nothing.

"Where's your homework book?' Kofo asked again.

Enitan said nothing and Kofo was angry.

"Where's your homework book? Or didn't you do your homework?' she shouted at her. Enitan nodded slowly. Kofo was surprised. This was most unlike Enitan Browne, the star pupil of her class.

Why didn't you do it?' she asked quietly, anxious to know what had brought this about.'I was washing my daddy's clothes, and I had to wash our toilet and bathroom,' Enitan replied, glancing at her feet.

'Agbepo!' Kenneth whispered audibly, and the whole class burst into laughter. Kofo saw red. Agbepo was the Yoruba name for night soil men and no child, or adult, liked to be called one of those.

'Shut up all of you!' she shouted at them. 'Kenneth, get up! Close your eyes and hands up!' She could not believe her ears. What were Enitan's parents thinking of when they asked her to wash her father's clothes, and their toilet and bathroom all in one evening? A little girl! Kofo wondered what her mother was doing while a little girl like Enitan was doing such adult household chores. She came to the conclusion that some people did not deserve children at all.

"What was your mummy doing when you were doing all these?" she asked Enitan. Enitan's lower lip trembled, and she looked as if she was about to cry. This was part of her plan to get Miss Odu to meet her daddy. It had been simple enough when she was planning it, but now it was getting increasingly difficult with every moment. Miss Odu looked very angry. Enitan had not been expecting such anger from the teacher. Oh, she expected her to be annoyed all right, but not as angry as this. She lowered her eyes again, staring at her fingers.

'Please, Ma, my mummy is dead,' she replied quietly. Kofo's mouth popped open. She had not realized. She had not known at all that Enitan's mummy was dead. It dawned on her then that she knew very little about these children in her class. Well, they had been together for just two months. 'I'm sorry, she said quietly. 'Since when was that?'

"Two days after I was born. That's why I'm called Enitan; Enitan replied. 'I see,' Kofo smiled. Enitan literally means someone of history?

It is a name given to a baby who was born at a time when a particular thing happened in the family. In this case, Enitan would always be used as a reference when talking about her mother's death. On a more serious note, Kofo asked, 'Who asked you to do those jobs?'

'My daddy,' Enitan said and prayed silently that this never got to her father's ears. He had not even known that she had done any of those jobs. And nobody asked her to do them. She had begged and begged Risi, their house-girl, to let her wash the toilet and bathroom. Risi had asked her again and again if she was sure she had no homework, and she had said yes. That was ages before her daddy came home.

After finishing the toilet and bathroom, she had started on the clothes but Risi came in and took them from her. When her father came home too, he asked her if she had any homework and she had said no once again. She knew she was telling a lot of lies but one lie just led to the other, and she could not help it. Anyway, they were in a good cause, so God would forgive her, she consoled herself. Her father hated people who told lies and he would have smacked her for this. He never let her do anything except wash plates, wash her clothes and sweep the room she shared with Joy and Risi.

'Didn't you tell him you had to do your homework?' Miss Odu asked quietly, looking Enitan straight in the eye.

'Yes I did, and he said I could do it later, but I was so tired that I fell asleep and forgot,' Enitan lied desperately. You would be tired, poor girl, Kofo sympathized with the little girl wordlessly. "I see,' she nodded. "And do you live alone with your daddy?" she asked Enitan quietly, again.

"Yes; except for my sister Joy, who is at school now and our housemaid Risi,' replied Enitan, afraid. She had not thought she would be cross-examined so much.

So what was Risi doing, when you were washing those places and the clothes?' Miss Odu asked again. Enitan could take no more. She suddenly burst into tears. Miss Odu put her arms around her and comforted her. 'Don't cry, Enitan,' she said soothingly. That's all right. Let's forget about it, but next time, do your homework before anything else, okay?

Enitan nodded, relieved that the whole thing was over and went back to her seat. After this Miss Odu took more interest in Enitan than in any of the other children in her class. And Enitan knew this and made the most of the opportunity. She gave her teacher the impression that she was not very well looked after. Sometimes she came to school with her hair in a bond, and if Miss Odu asked her why, she said there was nobody to plait it for her for free, and her father forgot to give her money to go and plait it in the market.

Kofo always felt so sorry for poor Enitan. Then she started coming to school in her Sunday shoes because, according to her, her school shoes had become too tight, and her daddy would not buy her a new pair. That was the last straw for Kofo. She was going to report to the Headmistress, she said angrily, but Enitan begged and begged her not to. Enitan knew that the Headmistress, who knew her father very well, would not believe this story. She would only ask her father and he would be surprised, because he had only just bought Enitan's school shoes three months ago. The shoes were lying at home, doing nothing. It was only that Enitan wanted Miss Odu to feel sorry for her.

Please see him yourself,' she pleaded with Miss Odu.

'All right. I'll give you a note for him to come and see me on Open Day, said Miss Odu, and after a brief pause added, 'Do you think he will come.

Yes he will come, said Enitan. But he is such a charming man. He'll be so nice to you that you won't believe all I've told you, she warned her teacher, saying it as a matter of fact. "I hope his charm doesn't work on me, " smiled Miss Odu and patted Enitan on the head. It was Thursday, and they were vacating for the mid-term Break at Santa Maria and most private schools in Lagos.

On Tuesday, they would resume and that was Open Day, when all parents came to the school to see what their children had been doing, so Miss Odu wrote a note beneath the typed-out invitation for Mr Browne,

'Dear Mr Browne,' she wrote, ' I'd be very much obliged, if you can make it a point of duty to attend this Open Day celebration, as I have some very important things to discuss with you about your daughter, Enitan, Yours sincerely, E.K. Odu."

Enitan was very excited when she got home that day. She was excited; one, because at last, her daddy was going to meet Miss Odu, and two, because Joy was coming home for the weekend also. She jumped into Joy's arms when the latter arrived. They hugged each other, as if they had not seen each other for months instead of a couple of weeks before. Enitan did justice to the biscuits and sweets her sister brought her. Joy settled down and when their father came home, he was happy to see her too. While he was eating, Enitan gave him her teacher's note.

'Hello, what's this?' said Tayo Browne as he opened the letter.

'Read it, daddy, and you'll see,' Enitan smiled.

Her father finished reading the note and folded it. Then he looked at both Enitan and Joy's puzzled faces and smiled.

"Well?' said Joy.

'Hum, well what?' her father countered.

'What is it about?' Joy asked.

'It's an invitation to Santa Maria's Open Day celebration,' her father smiled

'I know that, but what does the note beneath it say?' Enitan asked 'It says your teacher wants to see me, because you, Enitan, have been taking your friends, boyfriends, and won't listen to what your teacher says in class. And that….

'Daddy!' protested Enitan, interrupting him.

'Daddy, do you have to talk to her about boyfriends and such things?' objected Joy. 'She is only a kid, you know.'

'A kid, my foot. Enitan knows more than you and me together,' laughed their father. 'Daddy!' protested Enitan again and they all laughed.

On Open Day, all of the classes in Santa Maria school had something to show to the parents. Some staged plays, some cultural dances, others sing-songs and fancy dress parades. The boys set out their craft and handiwork on long tables, while the girls arranged their sewing. The parents also had a chance to see the 'Operation Feed the School' garden and farm, and the pottery was also displayed. They all enjoyed the experience.

After they had all been thrilled by these events, they were conducted round the class rooms by their children. Each child took his parents to his class, where his teacher would be waiting to show them their child's work, and talk to them about the child's progress. Enitan waited until there were not more than two sets of parents in her class before taking her daddy in to meet Miss Odu. Miss Odu had just finished talking to Mr and Mrs Audu, about how good the twins, Hamza and Hadeiza were, when she heard Enitan's small voice announce.

'Excuse me, Ma, this is my daddy?

Miss Odu looked up and the sight of this tall hunk of a man, took her breath away. Sure, she had been longing to see Mr Browne, and she had known he could not be that elderly but surely not this young either. He looked very young, nothing like a man who had another, teenage, daughter.

This man was very handsome. His blackness shone like polished ebony. He was tall and slightly built and had sleek black hair. She did not know why she was feeling as if there were butterflies in her stomach. Could it be that she had fallen in love with this hunk of a man at first sight? Not at her age! Love at first sight, if there was anything like that, only happened to starry-eyed, giggling, adoring young teenagers, not to people in their late twenties. She forgot her manners, as she stared at Enitan Browne's father.

He smiled at her, and exposed dazzling white teeth. Kofo could understand what Enitan, small as she was, meant by her father's charm. This man surely could win anybody's heart with that super smile, and she could not trust her feelings any more.

"Well, well. How do you do, Miss Odu?' smiled Mr Browne.

'How do you do?' replied Miss Odu in a small voice, and felt so stupid and shy in his presence.

'I'm glad I've met you at last,' said Mr Browne. 'I used to hear a lot about you, when you first took over Enitan's class, but these days, I hear nothing more about you, so I thought you were..' He left the sentence unfinished and shrugged. Then he laughed and Kofo found herself laughing too. 'Well, what has Enitan been up to? I hope she hasn't been taking other girls' boyfriends or has she?'

he asked, still smiling at Miss Odu and giving Enitan a special wink.

'Daddy!' protested Enitan, and wagged her little finger at her father.

'Of course not,' smiled Miss Odu. 'But it's such a long and confusing subject that I don't think we'll have time to discuss it fully here today? Well, that suits me fine because I'd really love to meet you again, Miss Odu,' said Tayo Browne. Then, tongue in cheek, and seeing the confusion and doubt written on her face, he added,

'Official discussions, of course!'

Miss Odu smiled and said nothing. She could not trust herself to speak. This man really is charming, she thought within her. Enitan excused herself and left them alone. Kofoworola Odu could feel Tayo Browne's eyes on her, and wondered why it made her feel so uneasy. Men were always staring at her, but she never felt this way. Sometimes when they admired her, it amused her and sometimes it annoyed her. But today, she did not know which she felt out of the two. It was as if she felt both tearing her heart apart, each clutching at one side of it.

Pull yourself together, Kofo. You are not a teenager. Stop behaving like a love-sick one, she admonished herself. She nodded and said quietly, 'Yes, Mr. Browne. Official discussions.'

'When do you think it is a convenient time for you?' asked Tayo

Browne, tongue in cheek again. He found this girl a very interesting person. He could swear that behind that cold exterior she put to the world, was a warm and bubbling personality. And though she looked so confident, so composed and self-assured, he could see her defenses crumbling under his gaze. He could see that she was confused and he wondered why she should be.

On his own part, he would not in a million years have realised that Enitan's new teacher could be so beautiful and chic. The other teachers, the ones he usually met, were nothing much to look at. But this girl could not pass by a virile male, without him turning back to give her a second look.

Like the proverbial hippopotamus, she deserved and received more than a passing glance. She was what you turned and looked at again and again. He knew that he wanted to see her again. Enitan had been full of Miss Odu for the first few weeks of the term, but then the stories about Miss Odu's beauty, poise and nice nature had suddenly stopped. He had never known why, and occasionally when it crossed his mind why they'd stopped, he had put it down to the fact that, the novelty had worn off, as children always do, and she had lost interest in the new teacher.

The new asked teacher was more beautiful than Enitan had made her out to be. I must see her again, he said wordlessly to himself; and was jogged back to the present by Kofo's clear bell-like voice. He had not realised she had been speaking.

Pardon?' he said apologetically, with a smile.

'I said I'm always free after school, but I don't know about you,' Kofo explained.

'Oh, don't worry about me. I want it to be convenient for you.'

'All right, what about Friday. I want it to be soon, because I'm very worried about Enitan,' said Kofo with a frown. Oh yeah? Mr Browne said and Kofo laughed. All right, Friday. But where? I'll tell you what. Why don't we make it a date? We could go out somewhere to discuss, you know ...' said Tayo Browne.

"No! No! I'm sorry but I can't ... protested Kofo vehemently, shaking her head. 'Why not? I mean, you aren't engaged or anything so... Just then, Miss Odu spotted Olubunmi Shode and her parents.

She knew from the impatient looks Bunmi was giving her that they were waiting to see her. She seized this opportunity to finish her conversation with Mr. Browne.

'Excuse me please, I must talk to the other parents. I'll be expecting you here at 2.pm on Friday, Mr Browne. It's been nice meeting you,' she said hurriedly.

'Same here,' replied Tayo Browne and held out his hand.

Kofo placed hers in his and noticed that he held her hand a second more than necessary. She felt a tingle, an irrepressible surge of joy thrill right through her body. She quickly drew her hand away, said, 'Bye-bye,' and escaped to sanity with the Shodes. He came over and had a polite little conversation with them, before going in search of Enitan.

He found Enitan playing with a little boy of about six, a very good-looking and healthy little boy.

'Hello, who have we got here?' he said, bending down to talk to them.

'Hello, daddy, I didn't know you'd finished. This is Bode, Miss Odu's son,' Enitan volunteered.

The smile froze on her father's face. So the charming Miss Odu, with her wide-eyed innocence, already had a child. How some people's faces could deceive one. He heard Enitan's voice as if from a far distance.

'Bode, this is my daddy?'

'Hello! Shake me!' said the little boy, holding out his hand.

Tayo Browne took the little hand and shook it warmly. He could see in this Bode, a very nice and well behaved boy and he liked him at once. Bode's father must be somewhere in the corner, he decided, and much as he would have loved to see Miss Odu again, he had better watch out. He did not want to get himself involved in an affair where a child was involved. He would just forget her. But who would have thought she had a son of this age, he wondered again, and why on earth was she not married?

As he drove home with Enitan, he found himself still wondering where Bode's father was and why they were not married. She appeared so nice that he refused to believe she was a free girl, who had got herself into trouble. He told himself there must be a story behind it. She looked to him like somebody who wouldn't give herself to a man, unless that man was important to her, and she was sure he would marry her. And from the way she was talking to the parents about her pupils, she appeared to be a dedicated young teacher, and he was sure she would not do anything to jeopardize her reputation.

"Now come off it, Tayo,' he chided himself as they got home.

"Why are you still thinking about her? The girl has a child, and the child must have a father. You don't want to get involved. Forget about her.'

Chapter 6

Tayo Browne came home on Friday, looking puzzled but happy after his meeting with Miss Odu. He had gone to meet her at the school at 2.00pm exactly as arranged. They talked for about an hour but got nowhere. He could not make sense out of what the teacher was saying. She was insinuating that Enitan was not being taken care of properly.

Now wait, Miss Odu, I don't think I know what you are talking about,' he said. I mean, Enitan seems neglected to me. It's as if she doesn't get proper care. Sometimes she comes to school late and..' Now, hold on. Surely she is not the only child who comes late to school occasionally?' he asked in surprise.

No, she isn't but hers is more than occasional. It happens almost every day. And there are a lot more things I want to find out,' explained Miss Odu, looking directly at him.

"Well, I'm all ears,' said Tayo Browne, more amazed than ever.

Then she had told him a whole lot of things that he had not been able to make out. She would not come out and say exactly what that rascal Enitan was up to at school. She only gave the impression that Enitan was more or less an uncared-for child, a little girl who needed the love of a mother.

He was inclined to agree with her about that, but the fact that she was neglected, he could not swallow at all. And he wondered why Enitan should go to school late so often. Santa Maria was just round the corner, only about fifteen minutes walk at most from their house, and Enitan was always almost ready, before he usually left home for work. He kept thinking about the whole thing, trying to figure out what was really happening, but he could make no headway out of it. He decided to watch Enitan from now on.

One thing, however, was clear to him. He wanted to see Miss Odu again. She had allowed him to give her a lift home, telling him on the way that she lived alone with Bode, and her mother was looking after him till she got back home. She had made no mention of either a boyfriend or a husband; and much as he had longed to ask her about Bode's father, he had not been able to do so since she wasn't much of a talker. He dropped her in front of her house but she did not invite him in. She thanked him for the ride and went in while he drove off, still thinking about her.

He now knew she was not living with a man, even though she had a child. A lot of his friends would have said all Lagos girls were the same, easy game, and he should not bother himself with her. He might have given someone else the same advice too, had it happened to someone else, but he was broadminded and fair enough to know that they were not all like that. There were a few exceptions.

And he really wanted to see this girl again, damn the consequences. He had thought about her a lot, though unwittingly, in the past few days and he knew that, until he was sure her heart was somebody else's, he wouldn't stop thinking about her.

Well, he decided, it did not matter if she had a child or not. She was still the same person and he was not going to bother about how she got herself pregnant, if there was nobody special in her life right at the moment. That was her past, and it was no business of his. It was the present and her future, if possible, he wanted to concern himself with.

He started taking Enitan to school by himself every morning in his car. Enitan did not like this but since it meant her daddy would be likely to see Miss Odu every morning, she had not minded much. So Enitan got to school early, and is always neat every day now, as she used to be before she got any ideas about Miss Odu. She was worried though because it seemed to her as if Miss Odu was avoiding her daddy. Every time he brought her to school he made sure he always took her inside her class, but they alway found the teacher absent. She was either in the staff room or somewhere else, never in the class before the school bells rang.

Enitan could see the disappointment written all over her father's face every morning. Then after he had been bringing her for about a couple of weeks, he stopped coming in with her. He just dropped her at the gate and went away. One day, he met Miss

Odu at the gate. She was just coming, and she got to the gate, as Tayo Browne stopped his car there. Enitan got out, and Bode, who was holding onto his mother's hand, left his mother and started shouting, as soon as he saw her.

'Mummy, there's Enitan,' he shouted, running to her and greeting her. Enitan smiled at him, and tickled him on the chin. Bode laughed and Tayo Browne came out of his car too. Enitan said, 'Bode, won't you say hello to my daddy? I'm sure you know him. Bode looked at Enitan's daddy, smiled and said, 'Good morning sir.

'Hello Bode. Good morning. How come you did not say "Shake me" today?' Tayo Browne greeted Bode, lifting him up high. 'Mummy says, I'm not allowed to say "Shake me" to grown ups. She says it's wude?'

'Is that so?" asked Tayo Browne, turning to Kofo, and greeting

Kofo nodded, smiled and greeted him. She was feeling shy again. There was something about this man that always got her unsettled, and made her feel so unsure of herself. She wished he would just go away and leave her to go to her class. The most disturbing part of the whole thing was that, whenever she was alone, she nearly always thought about him. She could not understand what was wrong with her. She knew that he was more than ordinarily interested in her, but she had no intention of having an affair with one of her pupils' fathers.

Enitan's father's voice jogged her back to the conversation.

"Oh, I'm sorry. I was far away,' she apologized. She hadn't realised he had been talking to her. "I was asking you if we could all go out together on Saturday' Oh, you don't have to bother. I mean, I don't want to spoil Enitan's day,' Kofo said. Oh no, I'd love to have you around, Miss Odu, and Bode too.

It would be much more fun,' said Enitan quickly, wishing and praying the teacher would say yes.
"Mummy, please say yes,' put in Bode, looking pleadingly at his mother."Okay then, if you say it's no trouble,' Kofo consented to uncertainty.

"It's no trouble,' Tayo Browne assured her, 'So we'll pick you both up at home. Is that all right? Kofo nodded.

Bode could talk of nothing but their outing with the Brownes all week. He was sure they were going to enjoy it. Enitan had told him that her daddy was full of fun and she knew Bode would like him very much. He kept asking his mom if his daddy was as tall as Enitan's daddy. Did he smack naughty children? Did he always take mummy out? Enitan's daddy always took Enitan and Joy out, and he would smack them if they were naughty.

Kofo answered so many questions before Saturday that, by the time Saturday actually came along, she'd caught the excitement fever from Bode.

On Saturday, the Brownes came, dressed casually. Enitan was in a white pair of shorts and a red halter neck top. Her father was casually dressed in cotton trousers and an American sports shirt.

Kofo and Bode were not yet dressed. It was around noon and she had just finished scrubbing her kitchen floor. She could guess from the way Enitan and her father were dressed that they were not going anywhere special.

'Enitan said it would be nice if we went to the Bar Beach,' Tayo Browne explained as they sat down in Kofo's small sitting room.

'That's why we are dressed so casually. She's got the car filled up with all sorts of things-buckets, spades and the like. I hope you don't mind?'

Kofo shook her head uncertainly. She did not want to go to the Beach. She'd been there only once since Bobo died, and she hadn't enjoyed it much. It brought back too many memories, and reminded her too much of the lovely times she used to have there with Bobo. But she was not going to disappoint Enitan and Bode.

She could see that they were both very excited and pleased about this, and they were chattering excitedly. I've got my bikini in the car,' Enitan was saying. 'Do you have any trunks?' 'Trunks?' Bode did not understand.

'Oh, that's what boys wear for swimming.' 'Swimming! No, I haven't. Mummy, can we buy something on the way?'

'That's all right, Bode. You can use any old pair of shorts. It's only girls who really need bikinis and swimsuits,' Tayo Browne interrupted. Kofo changed into a bright, floral, cotton dress and pretty low-heeled sandals. Bode wore a red T-shirt and a blue pair of shorts, and then they were off. Kofo sat silently beside Tayo, all through the journey to the Beach, and spoke only when one of the children asked her a question or spoke to her.

As Tayo drove carefully through the streets, she kept thinking of all the other times she had made this particular journey, and how Bobo always drove fast, making her catch her breath. She gave a faint smile at the remembrance of Bobo's fast way of doing things. Suddenly Bode tickled her ear from behind, and she turned back to look at him.

She smiled and he smiled back at her. His smile was so much like Bobo's that her heart lurched forward at the sight of him. She blew him a kiss and turned back to face the road. They enjoyed themselves thoroughly at the Beach. The children rode on horseback, and exclaimed delightedly at the thrill it gave them. They took instant snapshots and had an early dinner at the Federal Palace Hotel. Kofo could not help joining in the carefree atmosphere created by Tayo and the children. They screamed delightfully at everything they saw and picked lots of shells and raced each other to the Beach. It was late in the evening when they got back home.

Both Tayo and Kofo began at once to thank each other for a lovely day, and they both burst out laughing. Tayo was glad to see Kofo relaxing a bit with him. He knew there should be a warm personality behind that cold front she put to the world. He also knew she had a story to tell. When they dropped Bode and his mother at their house he asked Kofo if he could see her again, and very quickly, she became the Kofo he had first seen, shy, hesitant and uncertain. Gone was the gay, laughing girl he had been out with all afternoon.

'I don't know,' she began uncertainly. 'Well, I do know,' he said before she could finish. I'll call you tomorrow evening and we'll go out for a meal somewhere. "What about Bode?' she asked, stalling. He looked at her hard, and she turned her eyes away. Tayo glanced at the back of the car and saw that both children were watching them anxiously. He could not tell what was in their minds. Their faces, except for the tiredness they showed, were expressionless. 'Enitan, why don't you take Bode inside? I'm sure he is very tired,' he said smiling, and Kofo brought out her keys.

She tried to get out, but he took the keys from her and gave them to Enitan. Enitan took the keys, opened the car door and got out with Bode. Bode glanced at his mother and she smiled at him.

'It's all right, darling. I'm not going anywhere. I'll soon be with you,' she assured him. When Bode and Enitan went in, Tayo took hold of Kofo's hands and held them in both of his hands. He looked straight into her eyes. Their gaze met for a moment and Kofo turned away. She felt as if there was some heat coming out from his eyes and burning her face. 'Kofo, why are you avoiding me?'

The question jolted her. It was the first time he had called her by her first name. 'I am not avoiding you,' she protested.

"You are. Or should I say, why are you running away from love?

Have you had a cruel experience or something?' he asked.

'What makes you think that?' Kofo replied.

'Well, you've been trying all your best to see that I don't get anywhere with you. You know that I am interested in you, don't you?'

'Interested? In what way?' Kofo asked.

'Oh, stop stalling. You know in what way. If you aren't afraid of getting involved, you would have found somebody to look after Bode for you, wouldn't you? What is it? I'm sure you can tell me?' he asked patiently.

'It's only that I don't want to be hurt any more. I would really love to go out with you but I'm scared...' she said.

'Scared? Of what? I'm not going to eat you, am I? We're going to have a meal together. For heaven's sake, Kofo, I just want to know you better, that's all. Have you been so hurt once?' he asked, still looking at her. 'Yes, very much,' replied Kofo, the tears stinging her eyelids as she tried to hold them back. 'Bode's father?' Tayo asked, squeezing her hand and Kofo nodded.

'Did he let you down? It does happen you know, but you must put it behind you. Don't let it mar your future.'

'No! No!' Kofo shook her head. 'You don't understand. He was very nice. He did not let me down. He died a week before our wedding day.'

'Oh, I'm sorry. I didn't realise .. 'That's all right. A lot of people around here don't know. They probably think I'm a free girl when they see Bode.' 'Did he know about Bode?' Tayo asked. 'No. I didn't either, until weeks after his death. A lot of people said I should get rid of it; but I couldn't do that to Bobo's child. It was the only link I still had with him, and Bode looks so much like him that I'm glad I didn't.'

'Bobo.., was that his name? Funny. I never heard of that name before,' Tayo said. 'Yes, it's unusual. His real name is Tokunbo. Tokunbo Coker.

But his elder sister used to call him Tokunbobo when he was a baby, and somehow, he got stuck with Bobo.' 'I see. But you must bury the past, Kofo. I lost my wife too, you know, but I'm not brooding over her any more. I've put that sorrow way behind me. I'm sure Bobo would not have wanted you to grieve so much for him.' 'Yes, I know. But I can't help it. Everyone keeps telling me Bobo was a great one for living life to the full while you are alive.

But I just can't forget it, try as I may,' Kofo said, close to tears again.

'You must try, and I want to help. Please give me a chance, will you?' Tayo pleaded.

Just then Enitan appeared as if from nowhere. They had been so engrossed in their talk that they hadn't noticed her coming. At the sight of her, Kofo suppressed a scream. 'The children!' she gasped. 'I'd forgotten all about them.' Enitan looked at her and said nothing. She opened the car door, and limbed in at the back, before saying, 'Bode's waiting for you Ma.

Kofo smiled and apologised to Enitan. Then she turned to Tayo and said, 'Thank you for a lovely day. I must go now. I'll see you tomorrow.'

'It's I who should thank you for a lovely day. Does it mean the date is on?'

"What do you think?' Kofo asked him, laughing. 'What about Bode then?' Tayo wanted to know."I'll leave him with my mother. "Are you sure he's going to be alright? Kofo laughed. That's nice coming from you, She said. Yes it's alright. What time tomorrow? She added.

"Let's say 5pm, shall we? Yes, see you then. Bye Enitan. Bye Bye! Enitan said and her father started the car. " Kofo waved to them, and went inside as they drove away. Enitan was very silent on the drive home. 'A penny for them; her father said, after a while. He had been waiting for her to start chattering as usual. 'A penny for what?' Enitan asked, puzzled.

'For your thoughts,' her father laughed. Enitan laughed too. 'Do you really want to know?' 'Yes. Or I wouldn't be asking, would I?' I was just thinking that you seem to be getting on fine with Miss Odu.'

'Oh, were you indeed!' said her father, rather startled. "Yes, it does look like it, doesn't it? Don't you like the idea?' 'Me? I'm thrilled about it,' said Enitan. Then after a brief pause, she continued. 'I was only thinking about Joy, that's all

"What about her?' her father asked. "Well, she won't approve. Joy doesn't want another mummy,' 'How do you know?' her father asked her.

I know. I just know, that's all. Joy doesn't want another mummy. 'Nobody's talking about another mummy now. So we'll just have to wait a while, won't we?' said Tayo. But I thought you were going to marry Miss Odu. I mean, that's why you are going out with her, isn't it?'

'Enitan! I haven't said anything about marriage. I am merely going out with her because I like her, and I want to get to know her better. Understand? Oh I see, Eniitan said in a small voice "You don't see. It looks as if you like Miss Odu very much. Do you?'

'Yes, daddy. She's so nice.' Her father said nothing. After a few minutes, Enitan asked if she could ask a question. Her father said yes of course she could, so she asked in a small voice where Bode's daddy was.

"He's dead. He died before Bode was born,' her father informed her,

'So Miss Odu is a widow?' Enitan asked. "In a sort of way, yes," her father replied, "Then why isn't she called Mrs Coker? Bode is Bode Coker and I thought widows bear their dead husbands' names,' Enitan asked again childishly,

I didn't exactly say she was married, did I? You are too inquisitive, Enitan. It will do you more good to ask less questions, okay?' her father scolded her, 'You'll understand these things when you are older?

So she asked no more questions. She knew it was going to be of no use if she did, as he had closed that subject, Next day, Tayo Browne called for Kofo at a quarter to 5p.m prompt. Kofo was surprised to see him so early.

I know women,' he explained with his easy smile. 'I know how long it takes you to get ready. The quickest, the modest ones, need nothing less than fifteen minutes. Others take thirty minutes 10 one hour,' 'And you didn't know what category I fell into?' "That's right.'

Kofo laughed. She was almost ready. She had taken Bode to her mother, who had been surprised and pleased when Kofo had told her she had a date and could not take Bode along. She was pleased because she saw Kofo's eyes shining.

For the first time, she had a radiance in her face, and her mother knew she was beginning to put Bobo's ghost behind her, and was pleased for her. It had been a long time ago since she had seen that look in Kofo's eyes. Her father was out to one of his church meetings. Mrs Odu had asked Kofo about this person she was going out with, but Kofo had said he was just a friend, and there was nothing serious between them. She would say no more, so her mother had let her go.

Chapter 7

Kofo and Tayo went out to dine at the Bukka Floating Restaurant along Marina. They went and sat upstairs, where they could see the Harbour from the inside of the Restaurant, built like a boat and dancing on the sea. Bukka Floating Restaurant was a beautiful work of art, internally and externally. Kofo had not been in anything like it before, but Tayo told her that was what the inside of a ferry boat looked like. They sat down and as soon as they did, a cheerful uniform-clad waiter, grinning from ear to ear, appeared and asked for their orders. He was so anxious to impress that the thought made Tayo laugh.

'We haven't even studied the menu yet,' he told the waiter, who smiled, bowed and said he would be back in a couple of minutes, to take their orders.

'We serve some delicious African dishes here, sir, or would Madam prefer European dishes? I could recommend some of our specialities,' he offered, moving away. Kofo watched him go and laughed.

'Nice fellow, isn't he?' Tayo said, as they both took the menu and studied it. 'Dundu Oniyeri! I wonder what that is?' said Kofo, looking at Tayo. 'Search me,' he said, 'but if I can judge by the type of African dishes they serve here, it's going to be delicious. Shall we order it?

'Oh, I'm sorry, I didn't even ask if you would like European food instead' No I can never get them down my throat, not with those raw tomatoes, onions, lettuces, carrots and cabbages they slice most of them. I hate eating raw things,' Kofo smiled. 'That makes two of us,' Tayo smiled back at her. The waiter came along, and they ordered Dundu Oniyeri for two.

It turned out to be just as good as they had expected, thick slices of fried yam served with fried snail stew. The snails were left whole, just as they came from their shells and not chopped to pieces. They ate in silence except for when Tayo ordered two Chapmans and the silence grew as they sipped their drinks after the meal. Kofo, who was feeling very relaxed and content, you could see that Tayo was very uneasy.

She was surprised that he looked so nervous. He had looked so worldly-wise to her and she had presumed he was an authority on women and would make her feel like a nobody. She had always been the one to be shy when on a date. This was a new one on her, where the man she was out with was shy. She kept looking at him, and as he lifted his glass, his hands shook and he spilled some of his drink on the white lace tablecloth. Kofo smiled. He was as nervous as a teenager on his first date, and she had thought he was so confident. She wondered how she could put him at ease. Tayo spilled his drink a second time and looked at Kofo.

'I'm sorry,' he said. No problem,' Kofo replied. 'Just don't forget to include the laundry bill. Tayo looked at the tablecloth and laughed along with her. He could not understand why he was feeling this way with this girl.

He, who had always, prided himself on being a Don Juan with women, old and young. Well, he thought, you can't win them all. You are so nervous,' Kofo broke through his thoughts. I'm not,' protested Tayo and Kofo laughed.

'Yes, you are,' she insisted. 'Be honest with me. I know you are and it's catching, you know. I'll soon catch it.' relaxed now and wanted him to be the same. The reserved, quiet girl had now opened up, and was ready to laugh and talk with "To be candid, I really was. I can't understand it though. It's never happened before, not even on my first date with my first girlfriend.'

'Oh, yeah?' said Kofo, borrowing the phrase from him. Tayo laughed and said, 'Oh, yeah! I've always been very confident with my women.

'You seem to have been out with or should I say you seem to have known a lot of women in your time,' Kofo teased him. 'Well, I've been around for a long, long time, you know. I'm thirty six and I do get by? "You must do,' Kofo smiled. But I want to get to know you, to really know you because I like you very much. If I say I love you, you won't believe me, so I'll say I like you very much. I want you to be a special person in my life,' he said.

Kofo said nothing in reply and the silence lengthened between them.

"Well?' 'Well what?' "Why don't you say something?'

"I can't think of a suitable reply," she said frankly but they began to talk and Kofo told him all about herself, her parents, her life before she met Bobo and up till the present day. Tayo was surprised to know this was the first date she'd had ever since Bobo died. It was surprising to him that a girl could stay the whole of six years without male companionship. This was a special kind of girl, and he respected her for it: By the end of the evening, he knew that he had gotten somewhere with her.

When Tayo took her home to her parents' house to collect Bode, she asked him in. Her father, who was back from his meeting, greeted him warmly, and Kofo knew he was pleased with what he saw, Bode came running out to meet them. "Mummy, you were long, " he said, "Where did you go to? "We went to eat in a restaurant but like a boat, his mother told him; planting a kiss on his head,

Mrs Odu made sure she got her daughter into the room, so that she could talk to her. Kofo knew she had been dying to do this, right from the moment she walked in with Tayo, so she said, 'Well, mummy?" "Well what? her mother said, feigning surprise, Kofo laughed and hugged her. If i don't know you by now, then I'll never know yew. You're dying to know all about Tayo, aren't you?' she asked her "Well, you can't blame me, You are not the sort of daughter who brings men home every day so naturally i am curious. Bode tells me he has a daughter in your class, Is that right? Kofo nodded,

Her mother looked worried, 'Does that mean he is married. "No, he is a widower and he's got two daughters, Enitan, that's the one in my class and her elder sister, Joy,' Kofo explained. Her father came in just then and smiled at them. He could see that his wife was worried, "What's happening to my girls then?' he asked, putting an arm round each of them, and looking at his wife, She ignored him and went on talking to her daughter,

"How old is this Joy?' she asked. 'Sixteen, I think, Why?' Kofo replied, It was now her turn with her father to be puzzled. She could not understand what her mother wanted to know about Joy's age. "Well, a sixteen year old girl could prove to be difficult,"said her mother thoughtfully, Kofo stood, gaping at her.

"Whatever for, mummy?' she asked. 'As a step daughter of course, Kofo, She'll be used to sharing her father's love, with just her little sister and won't welcome you,' her mother explained.

'Sunbo! One step at a time. They haven't told you they have made any plans to get married yet, Kofo's father exclaimed, amused. Thank you, daddy. My dear mummy, I know I haven't had male companionship for so long but that doesn't mean I'm taking

Tayo's initial interest as an indication that it will lead to marriage, Kofo explained calmly to her mother.

Oh, but I know this is something special and different. I just feel it in my bones, Kofo, that this man is going to play a great role in your life,' her mother argued.

Kofo and her father both smiled and exchanged glances. They were both used to her mother's feelings in her bones. She had a sort of sixth sense, and could nearly always tell what was going to happen. It was only a pity that she had not been able to foresee Bobo's death, before it had happened.

"Well, I hope so. I sincerely hope so because I like that man,' her father agreed. I like him too but he is so sleek and smooth. You'll have a big job tying him down, my dear, 'Sunbo Odu warned her daughter. That's very encouraging, mummy, thank you. Now both of you, can we stop this conversation and remember we have a guest,' Kofo smiled, making for the door. Oh, yes. We have kept him waiting for too long,' her mother exclaimed, pushing her out of the way and getting out.

"Steady,' her husband said. 'He's got Bode for company.' For the first time in years, Sunbo Odu was really happy. She had seen that radiant light in Kofo's eyes again and she knew that her daughter was taking a second chance at happiness. All these years, she'd been so worried and sad at the thought that Kofo had taken Bobo's tragedy so much to heart. Even Bobo's family had buried the past long ago. She had tried so hard to introduce suitable young people to Kofo, and to get her interested in some social activities, but had not succeeded so far. Her husband was always telling her to leave Kofo to adjust herself in her own good time. But much as she loved Bode, she had longed for more grandchildren, and as Kofo's social life was non-existent, she had become very worried. It broke her heart to see Kofo withdraw into her shell more and more, coming alive only when she was with them or Bode, now working herself to death at school. She thanked God that Kofo was becoming her old self again.

The only cloud on the horizon, as far as she was concerned now, was Tayo's sixteen year old daughter. She was sure the girl was going to be a lot of trouble to Kofo. The little girl probably would give Kofo problems too, but it would not be difficult to win her over. She was in Kofo's class already and would know more about her than the elder sister. Her husband did not share her opinion. "How do you know, Sunbo? After all, you've never met either of these girls before; he asked.

"Well, I just know that's all. I'm a woman so I should know these things."'You may be right, but let's hope it won't be so. I'm sure this girl loves her father very much. If she does, she will be quite willing to accept Kofo, if only for her father's sake? This thought brought some comfort to Sunbo Odu's worried mind. 'I hope so but why did Kofo have to go and fall for a widower, and one who has children at that?' she complained.

'Sunbo! Are you forgetting that Kofo is more or less a widow herself, and she is an unmarried mother? You should thank your stars Kofo is so lucky to meet such a charming man,' her husband told her. 'Yes,' she agreed, 'and I'm happy for her. She deserves to be happy, our Kofo does. Oh God, I hope it's alright.' 'Don't worry yourself so much yet. You don't know that they are in love or…" I know my daughter, O.E, and she is in love. Kofo's going to be happy again. You mark my words.' 'O.E.' (standing for Oladapo Edward) smiled wryly and silently prayed that his wife was right. Kofo's life had been such a closed up one that he could not help being happy she was taking an interest in life again. But he did not want her to fall into the arms of the first man that came along.

He wished she could broaden her scope first. But even if she fell for this Tayo Browne, he, Oladapo Odu, would not mind much, because the man was mature and appeared to be nice. Her father loved Kofo very much, and even though he always appeared to be unconcerned about her, he was very much concerned. After all, she was his only daughter and the best of daughters at that. 'Dear God,' he prayed. 'Let it be all right for her this time.'

Chapter 8

Kofo and Tayo continued meeting almost every evening and she got to know him better. Kofo became once again the bubbling, warm personality Bobo had made her before his death. She came alive. Her eyes were once more sparkling, and it was clear to all who knew her that, at last, the sun was shining on her world once again. She was in love for the second time in her life and happy. When she went to see Bobo's parents, she told them about this new man in her life. They were very pleased. They had been as worried as her parents that Kofo had not been able to lay Bobo's ghost easily. They had watched her grow into a withdrawn, young woman, and felt sorry because they knew Bobo would not have wanted her to grieve for him so much. But there was nothing they could do. It was only Molara who could talk to her and find out what she really felt, but Molara was married now and lived in Zaria with her husband.

Mrs Coker had tried several times to talk to Kofo about going out more, mixing with people of her own age, instead of having only Bode and elderly people like themselves and her parents for company but her advice fell on deaf ears. She was grateful that Kofo was really going to be a woman again; and she had asked her to bring Tayo to see them. Kofo told Tayo she would like him to meet Bobo's parents, 'Well,' he said, 'I suppose I have to meet them sometime since I'm going to be Bode's stepfather. And now is as good a time as any. Kofo laughed but said nothing. Tayo took her in his arms and kissed her. You haven't said anything. I've just proposed to you. What's my answer?' he asked her.

'Do I take that as a proposal? Kofo looked at him, surprised.

Tayo nodded. "Or do you want me to ask you as a knight would ask a princess and with full formality?' Kofo laughed again. She was always laughing these days and everybody said it did her good. Tayo waited impatiently for her answer. He was sure it would be yes, but one could never be too sure with women. 'Don't you think it's rather too early?' Kofo asked him uncertainly. 'It's not too early. Time doesn't really matter. I've known you for four months now, and I know that you are the one I want. I'm old enough to know my mind.' "But I haven't met Joy yet and it would not be nice to spring the idea on her.'

I'll tell Joy. She's no problem. I know her,' Tayo said confidently.

Kofo pleaded with him to wait for some time before they actually arranged anything. Then they took Bode and went to see the Cokers. They were pleased to meet Tayo and made him very welcome. Bode, as soon as he saw his grandparents, started chattering away like mad. Mr. Coker and Tayo discussed politics, the nation's economy and each other's work, while Kofo and Mrs. Coker went inside to talk about even more serious things.

He is such a charming man, and young too. Did you say he is a widower?' Bobo's mother asked Kofo. Kofo nodded. I think he loves you. You should see the way he looks at you. You deserve to be happy, Kofo. I'm so happy for you.' 'Thank you,' Kofo smiled and hugged her.

Meanwhile, Mr Coker had turned the trend of conversion between him and Tayo to Kofo. He told Tayo about Bobo, how he died and how Kofo had grieved so much for him. He told him that both him and his wife were always glad, when they remembered that, short though Bobo's life had been, he had enjoyed life to the full and had always been happy. 'Kofo is a very good girl, 'said Mr Coker, very seriously. If you marry her, she will make you a good wife. I do beg you to be kind to her. She so much deserves to be happy.'

'You have my promise,' said Tayo, moved by the older man's obvious emotion. "You know she always comes to visit us?' continued Mr Coker.

'Just look at that! Most girls in her position would not even bother to bring Bode to see us often, let alone bring along their new boyfriend to introduce him.

Kofoworola is a special kind of girl. Our son made the right choice before his untimely death.' By the time they left the Cokers, it was apparent Tayo had been a great hit with them. They were sure he was going to make Kofo a kind and understanding husband, and Bode a good father.

Joy came home while her father was out. She became annoyed because she had come home twice the week before, and he had been out both times too. And it was with this same Miss Odu, Enitan's teacher. She could see from the way Enitan was bubbling with excitement that there was some news, so she asked her. Enitan told her that their daddy had been seeing a lot of Miss Odu.

"What's strange about that?' Joy asked. Joy, you don't understand. I think daddy is in love with her. He'll probably marry her.'

'Marry, my foot! She's just one of them-the aunties, you know. As soon as another one comes along, he'll leave her,' Joy said with a sardonic smile.

I don't think so, Joy. Miss Odu is very pretty, smart, elegant and nice. Enitan explained.So were all the others to you, Enitan, Joy said coldly, and walked out of the room. She knew her father, and was sure he was not going to marry again. He was content with just having girlfriends. She was not bothered by the fact that he had been seeing alot of this Miss Odu. He had seen a couple of women a lot of times in the past before dropping them. He did not need a wife and they did not need a stepmother, Joy told herself. She never wanted her father to get married again because then they would have to share him with another woman, and she would probably always get them into trouble with him, as her friend Toun's step mom was always doing.

It was very late when her father came home and she could not go back to school that very day. She decided to go back on Monday morning. She had become very tense as the hours moved on, and there was no sign of her father. When he finally arrived, one look at his happy face told her all she needed to know. He had enjoyed himself very much with this Miss Odu. It might be a real problem this time, she told herself. Her father greeted her warmly and asked her about school, and how she was preparing for her exams. He chatted on and on, asking her about everything, telling her stories and jokes everything in fact but the very thing she wanted but feared to hear.

He said nothing at all about Miss Odu so Joy relaxed. She had just been panicking for nothing, she told herself. Her father had no intention of getting married again. He was quite content with the way things were. She could see that he was genuinely interested in her plans, so she put the new auntie out of her mind and concentrated on telling him what was happening to her.

The next day, which was Sunday, she went to Church with Enitan, while their daddy stayed at home. He rarely went to Church, but he always made sure they did. He was one of those people who went to Church only on festive days. After Church, Joy went next door to chat with her friend, Sonate Pedro.

Sonate attended the Anglican Girls' Grammar School and was a day student. She was also in form 5 and was of the same age as Joy. They had been friends ever since the Pedros' moved in two in houses away from the Brownes. Mrs Pedro was always very nice to Joy and Enitan, treating them like her own children, and Joy never knew how Enitan tried to match-make between Mrs Pedro and their daddy. Sonate was a very good friend, kind, sympathetic and always anxious to please. She was an ideal friend-the best of friends, Joy always told her classmates. Though they were of the same age, Joy took all her problems to Sonate.

Nice though Sonate was, for some time now, Joy had been avoiding going to the Pedros because Sonate's brother, Tewiah, had been trying to get more than friendly with her. Until quite recently they'd all got on fine, Tewiah, Sonate and Joy. She had always looked on Tewiah as an elder brother and this change in their relationship had come as a surprise to her. Tewiah was a handsome, fun-loving, easy-going boy, who was loved by everybody. He helped his mother and sister quite a lot, and she liked him as a brother. She could not even begin to think of him as a boyfriend. He had actually spoken to her about it and she had refused. She had tried to give him some reasons why but they had stuck in her throat. Tewiah, being Tewiah, had laughed the whole thing off, and had continued to behave in as friendly a way as before towards her. But she has found it difficult to go back to that former carefree relationship with him. She was glad today that

Tewiah was not at home. He was away at boarding school too, getting ready for his 'A' levels.

She had a nice time with Sonate, and then they both went home together to Joy's house. She showed Sonate her love letters from her current boyfriend, Tunde Euba. Sonate read the letters with some feelings of misgiving. They were quite good of course, professing his undying love for Joy, but Sonate knew that it was just a matter of time before Tunde Euba would get fed up with her and move on to greener grass. Everybody except Joy, of course, knew that Tunde Euba was a great flirt. He regarded himself as God's gift to women, and though young, he knew he was very good looking and attractive to women of all ages. He used this to his advantage and had broken the hearts of a great number of girls. He wanted just one thing from them, and as soon as he had that a number of times, he promptly grew bored, cooled off little by little, and dropped them.

This Sonate had told Joy several times, but Joy would not listen. She thought Sonate was running Tunde down because Tewiah wanted to get on with her. So Sonate had learnt to keep her mouth shut where Tunde Euba was concerned. She finished reading the letters and gave them back to Joy.

Joy folded them across her breast and mused, 'Oh love! Oh fire!

What do you think about them, Nate?'

"Well, I suppose they are all right,' Sonate replied non-commitally.

'Nate! Is that the best you can do? Don't be so unromantic.

You've really got a chip on your shoulder about Tunde, haven't you?' Joy exclaimed.

'I'm not the one who has a chip on her shoulder about him. It's you,' Sonate protested. 'Look Joy, why don't we talk about something else? I'd rather not discuss him because he breeds arguments between us.'

'Okay, if that's the way you want it,' Joy said, annoyed that Sonate would not discuss something that was so important, so dear to her heart, with her. She put the letters away and sat down with a face as long as the day before yesterday, Sonate thought.

Sonate ignored her expression, though, and changed the subject.

"Where has your daddy gone to?' she asked Joy. 'To see one Miss Odu. She is Enitan's teacher, and according to Enitan, he's been seeing quite a lot of her, but Risi says he hasn't brought her home yet' 'Maybe he is serious about her then?' In what way? If you are thinking of marriage, then that is out

'Why? Your dad's a very handsome man, you know. He's not yet forty, is he? He's bound to think of marrying again some time.don't you think?' Sonate asked her and added excitedly, 'And it would be nice for you to have a mummy again.

'Look, Nate, I don't want a mummy except my real mummy

'What about Enitan?' Sonate asked.

I can take care of her. After all, we've managed so far without a mummy,' Joy said, feeling uneasy for no reason at all.

'But I'm sure your daddy needs a wife. I bet he's lonely,' Sonate persisted.

'Look Nate, why can't you get it into your head that he has us?

That's all he needs.'

'But you are only children. He needs adult companionship.'

'I am not a child. I am sixteen, going on seventeen.'

'I know. All right, take it this way, you want to get married to Tunde in future, don't you?'

'Yes, I do, but what has he got to do with this?' Joy asked,

'Well, when you do, Enitan too will be grown up then, probably in boarding school and leading her own life. Then your daddy will be all alone. You see what I mean?' Sonate explained.

Yes, now she understood. Damn this Sonate girl, Joy thought irritably. She had a way of making one see things in a different light. Now she felt unkind for not wanting her father to get married again but she definitely did not want a stepmother. I bet your mum's lonely too. Why don't we bring them together?' she asked sweetly, with an ironic smile.

'There's no need to be so sarcastic, Joy. I was only trying to help. You know my mum's a grandmother,' Sonate flared.

Joy felt unkind again and apologised. I'm sorry, Sonate, but I wish you'll believe me when I say my daddy does not want a wife. Just then a little boy they had both never seen before bounced in shouting, 'Enitan! 'Enitan!' They were surprised to see him. Sonate got up from Joy's bed and went to the door to bring him in.'Hello. Enitan's sleeping. Who are you?'

Hello. My name is Bode Coker. Are you Enitan's sister? Bode asked shyly.

No, I am Sonate. I live just along the road. That's Joy, Enitan's sister. Sonate explained. Bode looked at Joy and smiled. Joy smiled back at him. Who brought you here, Bode?' she asked him. Her father came in then and carried Bode up on his shoulder.

'So, you little rascal, you are here already.

Hello, Sonate. Hello, Joy. 'Good evening, sir,' Sonate said.

Hello, daddy. Did you bring him?'

I brought him and I'd like both of you to come to the sitting room and meet his mother. She's anxious to know you, Joy,' her father said, and walked out of the room with Bode.

Joy and Sonate glanced at each other. Joy got up from the bed and looked at Sonate again. She knew what her friend was thinking so she said, 'Don't ask me, Nate. I thought he'd gone out with Miss Odu. I don't know about Mrs Coker.' Kofo sat uneasily on the settee in the Brownes' sitting room. She could not understand why she was so nervous. She wished Enitan was here to give her moral support. Tayo had said she would like Joy. But of course she knew that she would. She would love anything that was his. But what would Joy think of her? She looked around at the sitting room. It was so luxurious. She had not expected such luxury and it gave her a jolt to see Tayo's beautiful home. Everything here spelt money and was spick and span. She wondered what they were all doing inside, leaving her sitting here alone.

Bode ran in and shouted. 'Mummy, I've seen everywhere and Enitan's sister!' Kofo laughed and tickled his chin. She wished she had a child's uninhibited confidence. He would not even notice if anyone disliked him, but anyway Bode was so adorable, everybody liked him. Tayo came in, followed by a girl Kofo knew instinctively could not be Joy. She wondered who this was for a moment, but on seeing the tribal marks on the girl's face decided that it would be the maid. Tayo sat down next to her, and introduced the girl.

"Kofo, this is Risi, Risi, this is Enitan's teacher, Miss Odu. I want you to look at her well, because you'll be seeing a lot of her. Risi knelt down on both knees and greeted Kofo warmly with a smile. Kofo greeted her too, and she got up to leave as Joy and Sonate came in. One look at them and Kofo knew that the taller one of the two was Joy. Though Tayo had said she looked exactly like her mother, she had something of her father and Enitan in her. Tayo glanced at Kofo and saw how nervous she was. He caught hold of her right hand and held it in both of his hands.

'Relax, Kofo. They are only children. It's going to be alright, he whispered and Kofo shot him a grateful look and smiled. Sonate and Joy both greeted Kofo politely. They were both surprised to see somebody so young and chic, but this was far from what Joy had expected. This lady looked nothing more than twenty-five, and could hardly be taken for the mother of this lively little boy. Kofo had her hair styled and was putting on Iro and Buba with a pair of simple Indian slippers, yet she looked like somebody out of a film. Sonate stared at her, while Tayo Browne made the introductions.

'Kofo, this is Joy, and that is her friend, Sonate Pedro. She lives two houses away from us here. Joy and Sonate, this is Miss Odu, Enitan's teacher.

Kofo smiled uncertainly at them and said, 'I'm pleased to meet you both. I've heard so much about you, Joy, that I feel I know Joy said nothing and kept a wooden face. Sonate smiled back at Kofo. She liked this pretty woman. She looked so nice and friendly, with a warm and affectionate nature. And Joy's daddy was looking at her so lovingly that they knew he must be feeling very lovely toward her. Joy took one look at her daddy's face as he looked at Kofo, and knew that she had a battle on her hands.

This time it was the real thing. Her father had fallen in love again. No wonder, Sonate thought. This woman was as nice as she was pretty. Such a warm and lovely smile too. Joy said nothing. She just stared past Kofo as if the latter was not there at all. Kofo knew instinctively that Joy did not like her. She was not actually unfriendly outright, but she had registered the fact with Kofo, in those few minutes, that she was not welcome. Kofo was impressed by Joy's beauty though. At sixteen, she had all the assurance of a woman of twenty-one. Kofo felt a little daunted by this reception, but she had half expected it, so she said nothing. Tayo, too, was surprised by Joy's coldness. She always tried to be polite and nice to his girl friends in the past.

As the girls went out, Kofo said, 'Joy's a beauty. She looks so confident and grown up. And Sonate is a nice girl.?

Tayo said he thought Enitan would be a lot prettier than Joy, once she lost her babyish fat and Kofo agreed with him. At the mention of Enitan, Bode started asking for her again. So Tayo told him to go and wake her up.

Joy was fuming as she sat in their room. Sonate looked at her, and knew what she was thinking but said nothing. 'I won't stand for it!' Joy said under her breath, but a little too audibly, for Sonate heard her. "You won't stand for what?' 'You know what, Nate.

Why? She's no more than a girl herself and an unmarried mother! I don't see what daddy wants with her,' Joy stormed.

"Well, unmarried mother or not, I think she is beautiful and she's nice too. I'm sure if you get to know her "Thank you,' Joy broke in. I know it is gratifying to watch the antics of a lunatic, but harrowing to have him as a son.? then I'll go ahead and humour you...'

'I don't want you or anyone to humour me. I'm not a child; broke in Joy.

'Then stop behaving like a spoiled one. One does not, when engulfed with great bitterness and sorrow, blind one's eyes with tears. You should be able to see that your dad loves her and she appears to love him too,' Sonate explained patiently. 'Anyway, I still insist that I don't want anybody to take my mother's place. I won't allow it,' Joy said passionately. But she won't take your mother's place, not in your heart anyway. There should be room in your heart to love a lot more people than you do already,' Sonate said gently. She could understand how Joy felt, but she wanted her to see things as they really were. I'm not talking about me. I'm talking about daddy and Enitan. They will soon forget my mummy,' Joy snapped impatiently at her friend.

Joy, you ought to be happy for your daddy. He seems to be so happy now. I'm sure Enitan would love a new mummy. After all, she never knew your mummy. And your mummy is dead. This woman is alive. Enitan will love the memory of your mummy and this woman too. Children are resilient, you know?' Joy felt angry with Sonate again. Why did she always have to be so right? She wished she could be able to put Sonate in the wrong too one day- just once. She would be pretty glad to. Sonate knew how Joy was feeling so she tried to soothe her. 'Anyway, nobody has said anything about marriage yet, so why don't we shelve the matter for now?' she said soothingly.

Joy said nothing and just then Bode came in again. They both looked at him as he stood uncertainly at the door. 'Where's Enitan sleeping, please?' he asked in a small, wobbling voice.

'Come on in. She is over there,' said Sonate, pointing to Enitan's little bed in the corner of the room. Bode came in and rushed straight to Enitan's bedside. He beat her legs gently and shook her. Enitan opened her eyes and blinked as she recognised him. Bode!' she shrieked delightedly. Who brought you here? When did you come?" "My mummy and your daddy,' the little boy laughed at the surprise on her face. Enitan scrambled out of bed as quickly as she could and then she saw Joy and Sonate. 'Oh, hello, Joy. Hello Sonate,' she greeted them.

Hello, Enitan!' they both replied. 'Have you met my teacher?' she asked them. "Yes, we have,' smiled Sonate. 'What do you think about her? Isn't she pretty?' Enitan asked excitedly. 'Beauty lies in the eyes of the beholder, my dear Enitan,' Joy said sardonically, annoyed that this lady's beauty was to be brought into their conversation again. 'But you must admit that she is beautiful, Joy,' Sonate said reproachfully. 'Oh yes, she is. She is the most beautiful teacher in our school," Enitan added. 'And I bet she is nice too,' Sonate put in. 'Ah, the nicest Sonate, Everybody likes her. You'll like her too,

Joy,' Enitan said, standing up for her teacher.

"Spare me, both of you. I've heard enough of the great Miss Odu's virtues for a day and if you don't mind ...' She left the sentence unfinished, and nodded towards Bode. Both Sonate and Enitan had forgotten Bode's presence in the room, They both looked at him and saw that there was nothing on his face to show whether he had understood what they had been saying, Sonate was glad Bode was too young to understand Such a jeering remark, if repeated to his mother, would hurt her very much. Enitan pulled his hand and they went out of the room together.

Joy left with Sonate shortly after. She had no wish to go to the Pedro's a second time, but she could not bear to be in the same house with her daddy and his new family. She spoke neither to Bode nor to Kofo. She just told her daddy she was going home. Her father, hurt though he was by her unfriendliness, could not very well refuse her. He had noticed Joy's cool and distant attitude towards Kofo and Bode, but he said nothing. He did not want to antagonize her by not allowing her to go where she pleased.

Kofo, on her part, knew that Joy was glad to get away from them. Nevertheless, she and Bode had enjoyed themselves very much and she tried to put Joy out of her mind for the moment, when Tayo took them home. Bode chattered as usual on the way home, telling Enitan, who accompanied them, that he liked Sonate and Risi more than he liked Joy, and how pretty everybody was.

Kofo was silent, her mind preoccupied with all sorts of thoughts; and Tayo knew that she was worried. He said nothing, just squeezed her hand, and smiled at her. Tayo Browne took Kofo to meet all his family and friends, and they all liked her. She was so pleasant and nice that no one could wish for a better wife for Tayo. They all said he was very lucky to meet someone young, pretty and kind. She was always so polite and courteous to everyone.

Even Shade, Tayo's elder sister, and Tayo's mother, who had got on well with Tope, Joy's mother, had loved her when they first saw her. They had frowned on the fact that she had had a child out of wedlock, when they first heard about it, but Tayo told them how it happened, and they had felt sorry for her.

As for his other sisters and cousins, they were so pleased he was getting married again at last that they loved Kofo even without having ever met her. They did not even question the fact that she had already had Bode. They just welcomed her with open arms and hearts.

Joy could find no one on her side. Even her grandmother could find nothing wrong with Kofo. Her maternal grandparents, too, thought Kofo was just what was needed to make Tayo, Joy and Enitan lives complete. After that first meeting, she always avoided Kofo. She never said more than a civil greeting to her, but as time went on, she talked more to Bode and liked him.

Kofo was very worried about this. She did not know why Joy would not talk to her at all. She knew that Joy must have loved her mother very much. She did not want Joy to forget her mother or any such thing. She knew that she could never begin to take Joy's mother's place, and she did not wish to. But she wished Joy would give her a chance to make Tayo happy. Joy probably thought Kofo wanted to marry Tayo to give Bode a secure home.

The disgust and disapproval Joy felt was naked in her eyes. She always looked straight past her whenever Kofo came to their house. Kofo talked to Tayo about it, expressing her fears that Joy might never accept her.

'You'll have to be patient. Remember Joy was always very close to her mother,' Tayo explained, more worried than he wanted to admit. 'She took her mother's death very much to heart. Still, she's an affectionate girl and I'm sure she'll get to love you in time.'

Kofo looked unconvinced.'She isn't as unfeeling as she pretends to be,' Tayo went on. 'All the others in the family think the world of you, so why should you worry so much about Joy alone?' 'But Joy's the most important,' Kofo argued. 'She should be my greatest ally. The whole success of our marriage depends on what Joy does.' 'Oh, come on. You're exaggerating Kofo. That isn't like you. Anyway, she'll come round,' Tayo insisted. 'I know my own daughter. Don't worry.' Kofo signed and gave up trying to convince him hoping he was right.

Chapter 9

It was a long vacation and everyone was home for the holidays. Joy was glad to be home but she soon noticed a certain lightheartedness about her father that was not there before. He seemed like a new person altogether, and she knew it was due to Miss Odu. Both Enitan and Risi had hinted to her that they were planning to get married. Her aunties, grandparents and other relatives could talk of nothing else but Kofo and when Tayo would marry her. But her daddy had not actually come out and told anybody in so many words when it would be. Joy hoped fervently, however, that it was not true. She prayed something would happen to bring an end to the affair.

She could not think of her father remarrying. But he spent more and more time out of the house, and talked about Miss Odu and her son too often for Joy's comfort. It was always 'Kofo said this' or 'when Bode said that' or 'Kofo did that' or 'Bode did this.' The same thing happened too with Risi and Enitan. By the time Joy had been home for three days, she felt she would scream if anybody mentioned Bode or Kofo again, but she could not very well tell them so. For the first four days after Joy came home, her father kept dropping hints about the décor in the house needing a woman's touch, and how nice it would be to have the patter of little feet about the house again, and how nice it would be for Joy to have an adult to discuss all her girlish problems with.

Joy suffered all these hints but the last in silence. She would just make a non-committal reply, afraid that if she pursued the subject further, she might hear what she did not want to hear. But to the one that she needed female company for girlish confidences, she told him that she was all right with Mrs Pedro.

Sonate's mother was like a mother to her, she had declared. But her father had argued that she could not continue going along the road whenever she had problems, and anyway, what if the Pedros moved houses. Joy had said nothing but had thought to herself that she would rather die than confide in Kofo. Kofo was hardly suitable for the role of adviser on moral problems anyway, she said to herself.

On the fifth day after she came home, she was at table with her father and Enitan, eating their breakfast, when their father dropped the bombshell. 'Enitan and you, Joy, how would you like to have Kofo as your new mummy and Bode as your brother?' he asked them brightly, looking intently at first Joy, then Enitan.

Joy held the knife she was using to butter her bread suspended in mid air, and stared at him. She had known this was coming, but when it came, it was still a shock to her. She wondered for the umpteenth time how her father could be thinking of marrying this woman he met just some six months ago. Enitan also stared at her father, her face lighting up with pleasure. This was all she ever dreamt of coming true. They both could not find words to express their different feelings.

'Well, what do you say about it?' Tayo asked his children with mixed feelings.

He knew that Joy was floored and he was sorry that she felt that way about his love for Kofo, but there was nothing he could do.

Joy was a big girl now, and she had her own life to lead. He would be very foolish to give up Kofo just because one of his daughters did not approve of him marrying again. He knew that Enitan would be delighted and she was the one who found her voice first.

Daddy, do you mean that you and Miss Odu are getting married?' she asked in a shrill, excited voice. Yes Enitan we are, he told her.

Oh, daddy! I am so glad! It's my dream come true! Enitan exclaimed excitedly.

She got up quickly from her chair and gave her father a tight bear hug, and a smacking kiss on the cheek. She ran to Joy and then started hopping about excitedly, first on one leg and then on the other leg, as she always did when she was excited. Oh Joy, isn't it super? She cried delightedly.

Joy ignored her and, her face expressing no emotions, said in a low voice, 'Congratulations, daddy. I hope you'll be happy'

'Congratulations, daddy!' echoed Enitan.

'Thank you. Of course, I'll be happy,' their father answered with a grin.

He could see that Joy was not at all happy. He hadn't realised the intensity of Joy's feelings on this matter. He had thought that Joy was only upset because a change was going to take place in the household. But now, he could see, from the anger in her eyes and her expressionless face, that she was jealous of Kofo and disapproved of her. It looked to him as if she resented the place Kofo was going to take in his heart and in their household as a whole. So far she had been the mistress of the house. She probably thought Kofo's arrival would mean her receiving orders instead of giving them. He decided that he would talk to her later, and find out what she really felt about the whole affair. He wished she could be happy for him, though.

As soon as they finished eating, Joy announced that she was going to see Sonate. Her Father said nothing. Enitan looked surprised. She could feel, small though she was, that the atmosphere was tense. She looked first at Joy, then their daddy.

He shrugged his shoulders and Enitan said nothing. Joy went away to tell Sonate the 'latest.' When she got to the Pedros' house, she met Tewiah outside the house, cleaning his brother, Vojo's, car. He looked up as she came into their compound.

'Hello, Joy. Long time no see!' he greeted her.

'Hello,' Joy said in a low voice. 'Is Sonate in?'

"Yes, she's in the kitchen with our Ma. Hey Joy, what's wrong with you? He was surprised to see her so low. Nothing whispered Joy, close to tears and fled into the house before he could start asking more questions.

She found Sonate helping her mother to bake some queen cakes.

The tears started trickling down her cheeks as she saw them. She sat down on a chair and started crying bitterly.

"What is it, Joy?' asked both Sonate and Mrs Pedro at the same time, in alarm.

"Oh, Nate, he's told us! He's going to do it!' cried Joy.

"What's that? Who's going to do what?' Mrs Pedro asked, confused.

I know what she's talking about, Ma. I know,' said Sonate to her mother. Then she sat down by Joy and put her arms around

But Joy, you knew it was coming. Why are you so upset?' she asked Joy softly.

111

'Oh, Nate, it's so soon and so difficult to bear when it finally happens. Now she's going to order me about,' Joy wailed.

Now, now, Joy dear,' said Mrs Pedro soothingly, coming into the picture. I'm sure she won't be a bossy sort of woman. Your dad is not the type to bring in a woman who won't love you or will try to push you around, you know that.'

'Yes, she's not like that,' put in Sonate. 'I've met her and she is nice. If only you can accept her, Joy, ...'

'Accept her? It's easier said than done. How can he do that to my mum's memory?' cried Joy, her whole body trembling with sobs.

Now, Joy, you know your dad has tried. Your mum died almost ten years ago. That's a lifetime—Enitan's lifetime. A lot of men can't wait that long, and I'm sure your dad did so because of you and Enitan,' Mrs Pedro said.

"Or, Ma, to be more precise, because he had not found somebody worthy of taking your mum's place until he met Miss Odu. Try to see it that way, Joy. She is just right for him,' Sonate pleaded.

'But I thought he loved Enitan and me. I thought he was quite happy with us, Joy wept. Now listen. Joy your daddy loves you both very much I'm sure and you know it, my dear. But you are his children. You can't take the place of a woman in his life. The sort of love he has for you is quite different from the love he has for this woman. He doesn't love you any less because of her. There are different places in his heart for you all. And I'm sure he wants more children. Don't you want a little brother or another little sister too?' Mrs Pedro paused, to see Joy's reaction.

Joy, still sniffing into her knuckles, did not look up.

Mrs Pedro went on. 'Joy, I'm talking from experience. You will understand what I'm going to say better when you are older. A man needs a woman, and a woman needs a man as the years go by.

You need to give the love in your heart to somebody and to take in theirs, but most of all you both need just the companionship-the joy of being together. Your dad is only human and he needs the love, companionship, care and presence of a woman in his life.

You will grow up one day, so will Enitan, and get married and live away from him. Then his life will be very empty. He will be lonely and you'll probably find him a burden to you. But if he is married, his life will be fulfilled and he won't need to bother you much. Think about it, Joy, and try not to make him feel he's doing the wrong thing, because if you were to consider his happiness and Enitan's, you'll know that he is doing the right thing. You are grown up now,' she finished.

By this time, Joy had cleaned her face and was ready to take Mrs Pedro's advice. But, deep in her heart, she knew that Kofo could never take her mummy's place. She remembered her mummy as vividly as if it was yesterday. They had been very close, Joy and her parents. They took her to lots of interesting places and bought her all sorts of things toys, books, clothes and so on. Her mummy used to play games with her and teach her to sing songs and to dance. She also taught her lots of nursery rhymes, and always carried her, calling her 'my baby' until she became pregnant again. She remembered clearly her mom telling her that the swelling tummy was carrying a little baby sister or baby brother for Joy to play with, cuddle and look after.

Her mummy always took the pains to explain everything to her.

Soon her mummy had to go and stay in hospital, and her daddy used to take Joy to see her.

Then one day, daddy told her mummy had brought her a baby sister to play with. Joy, delighted, was taken to see the baby. Oh, mummy,' she said, still gazing at the tiny baby. 'She's so small! She isn't a bit like Doris's sister. That baby's so big and beautiful.'

"All babies look like this,' said her mother's faint voice. 'She'll soon grow. She'll have good food and care. You'll see. She'll grow up fast.'

Joy looked away from the baby at last and stared at her mother.

You're not really going to die, are you, mummy?' There was silence. No one in the hospital room knew what to do.

I heard auntie Shade say so but I don't believe her,' Joy told her mother but her expression was even more anxious. She was waiting too long for reassurance.

The others were still lost for words but her mummy smiled at her and told her that she was going to Heaven very soon to be with God because He wanted her there.

I want to go with you, mummy,' Joy had cried, clutching at her mother's thin hands.

No darling, God wants only me now. Some day, when you are older than grandma, he will take you. But now, he wants you to stay here and look after daddy and your little sister. Joy, always look after your sister, do you hear?' her mother had told her weakly with tears in her eyes.

Then she kissed Joy on the head and said, crying, 'God bless you, my darling' and daddy and the nurses had taken Joy out.

That was the last she saw of her mother but she had not forgotten, even though it was long ago. Soon afterwards (she now knew it was only two days later) her daddy had told her that her mom had really gone to God. And she had Kept that promise to look after really gone to God. And she had kept that promise to look after Enitan and her daddy. Now, it was through no fault of hers that. the promise was to be broken.

She cheered up and helped Sonate and her mother.

Tewiah came in and said he was going on a test drive in the car, and would like to come along.

Joy shook her head. No. I wouldn't.'

'Am I so repulsive to you?' Tewiah asked jokingly, with a twinkle in his eyes.

'Don't talk nonsense! You know it's only because I'm not in a mood to go out,' Joy reproached him.

'All right, whenever you are in the mood, I mean if ever you change your mind, remember I'm the first in line,' Tewiah said.

'Come on, Tewiah, leave Joy alone. She doesn't want to go out with you, so get off,' his mother laughed, shoving him out of her kitchen.

By the time Joy went back home, she had made up her mind that she need not be friends with Kofo. She would be polite to her. She would say no more than was necessary to her. She would give her no chance to get to know her better. She made up her mind also that, until her results were out, she would look for a job so that most of the time, she would be away from home and she wouldn't always have to see them. She slept soundly, having decided this.

A couple of days later, Kofo came to the Brownes' house with Bode. She was told by Risi that Tayo was out, but both Joy and Enitan were in. Kofo decided she would come in and wait for him. When Risi went to tell Joy and Enitan. who was there, Enitan rushed out delightedly to greet them. She greeted Kofo excitedly and sat down by her to talk to Bode.

'Daddy went to auntie Shade's place. He'll soon be back,' she informed Kofo.

Kofo had met auntie Shade and they had got on well instantly, much to everyone's surprise. Shade was older than Tayo by about five years and loved him very much. She was a strict and fussy woman, with an overbearing attitude towards everyone younger than herself. People seldom got on fine with her because she loved organizing other people's lives. She had taken to Kofo instantly, however and felt like mothering her. Kofo liked her too.

"Where's Joy?' she asked Enitan.

She's inside,' Enitan replied, and to cover up for her sister not coming out to welcome them, explained. 'She's reading, but she said she'll soon come out to greet you.'

'Let's go in and greet her, Bode, so she won't bother to come out again,' Kofo said cheerfully, getting up. She took Bode by the hand and said, 'Enitan, you lead the way to your room for us, please.'

Enitan's heart skipped a beat. Joy was only reading a novel. It would have cost her nothing to come out and greet Kofo, but she did not want to. Enitan could not understand why Joy was so hostile to Miss Odu, who always tried to be nice to her. She would not discuss Kofo or her relationship with their daddy. She would not talk of the wedding. Enitan saw no reason why Joy should not be happy about it, since it was making daddy so happy. They went inside and found Joy lying down on her bed reading. Kofo knocked on the door before going inside.

'Hello, Joy. How are you?' she asked brightly.

Joy barely looked up from her book and said, 'Hello.' Then she went back to reading her book.

Kofo felt snubbed. Her heartbeat quickened but she decided to brave it and continued talking to her. 'What's that you are reading?' she asked Joy.

'A novel,' Joy replied, eyes still on the book.

I know it's a novel,' Kofo persisted. 'It's the name of the novel

I'm asking you about.

'I see,' said Joy coolly. '*It's Speak to me of Love.*'

"Who wrote it?' Dorothy Eden. I've never read any of her books. Is it very interesting? Kofo asked brightly

Yes, Joy replied

I love novels too and I have a lot. I'll bring you some, Kofo offered, looking at Joy.

'Thank you, but don't bother,' Joy said, coldly and rudely.

Kofo felt as if she'd been slapped. She could see that she would have a big job getting through to Joy. She felt she must talk to her. She had not had an opportunity to talk to her, heart to heart, to see how she felt about the coming marriage.

'Enitan, can you take Bode out to the sitting room? I want to talk to Joy.'

'All right. Bode, come on,' said Enitan, holding out her hand to Bode and they went out.

Joy sat up on her bed and looked defiantly at Kofo. 'What do you want to talk to me about?' she asked her.

I suppose your daddy has told you we are getting married,'

Kofo began slowly.

'Oh yes,' Joy said. 'Congratulations— I forgot.'

'Thank you,' said Kofo. 'But, Joy, aren't you happy about it?'

'Me? What has it got to do with me? It doesn't matter how I feel. My feelings don't count in this matter.'

'They do, Joy. They matter a lot to me. I want to know how you feel,' Kofo persisted.

"What for? It won't change anything,' Joy said.

'I want to know because we are going to live together and I want us to be friends.'

'Well, if you must know, I am not happy about it. I can never be friends with you. You want to take our mom's place. You want to take daddy's love from us. I hate you!' Joy said passionately.

Kofo was shocked at Joy's outburst. So this was the intensity of Joy's feelings for her. She remembered how glad Bode was when she told him Enitan's daddy was going to be his new daddy. He had jumped around excitedly, asking if they were going to live in Enitan's house now. He had been very happy at the thought of having Joy and Enitan as sisters. But if this was how Joy felt, Kofo was not sure any more that she wanted to go on with this wedding.

Joy, I'm sorry you feel this way about me. I want you to know that I have no intention of taking your mother's place. I know I can never do so. I love your daddy and I want to make him happy, that's all and Oh!—I suppose whatever explanation I give, it won't satisfy you. But I want you to bear this in mind. The love between your daddy and me makes no difference to the way he feels about you and Enitan. I'll be going now,' Kofo said and got up.

'Bye bye!' Joy said rudely.

Kofo looked at the young girl on the bed for a minute and then walked out of the room. She stayed in the sitting room chatting with Enitan and Risi for a few minutes, before leaving with Bode. She left a message with Enitan and Risi for Tayo to come and see her. That night, alone with Bode at home, she thought and thought about it and knew that she could not go through with it. She was not going to marry Tayo Browne, not if Joy felt this way about her. Tonight, she would break off with him.

Chapter 10

Tayo Browne, on his way home from Kofo's house, thought the bottom was falling out of his world. He had just been told to leave her alone, and she would not say why, except that she thought it would not be a good idea, after all, if they got married, since his grown up daughter was so much against it. She would not come out and tell him exactly what had happened between Joy and her, to spark off such a dreadful decision. She had answers to all his arguments, and much as he pleaded with her, she would not change her mind. He had not realised that Kofo could be so firm and stubborn. Damn Joy! Heaven knows what had happened between them. Why couldn't the silly girl realise that she could not take the place of a woman in his life?

Maybe he had left it too late himself, that was why Joy was finding it so difficult to accept Kofo. Maybe he should have married again long ago before Joy was a grown woman but damn it, he had not met anybody like Kofo earlier-somebody he loved.

Or Joy was probably thinking Kofo would upset all their lives.

Oh women, however small they are, they always manage to give you problems he brooded, his head full of whirling thoughts.

Joy was probably thinking he had forgotten her mother and was going to give her place to Kofo. But how could he ever forget

Tope, especially with Joy growing more and more like her every day? He could never forget her but how was he going to tell Joy that the emotion he felt for Kofo, was quite different from the feeling he had had for Tope? He had loved Tope with the passionate, reckless love of the young, but Kofo he loved with a mature, warm, understanding love.

With Kofo, it had been almost love at first sight, but with Tope, it had been very different. He had known Tope almost all his life, but he hadn't liked her because she was so sickly. She lived with her parents, in the same house as his auntie, but she was nearly always in and out of hospital, when they were children. He was only two years older than she was and very rascally, but Tope had been very skinny, small for her age and over-protected. He had always told his sisters and cousins that he did not like that skinny girl upstairs, whenever they had gone to spend holidays, or visit their auntie and her family. His cousins, especially Kemi, who was Tope's closest friend, always told him that she was a very nice girl. He barely talked to her when he saw her.

Then he had gone away to Ibadan for his secondary school education, and his auntie had moved away from Montgomery Road. So he did not see Tope again for a very, very long time and he had promptly forgotten all about her.

Then it was Kemi's sixteenth birthday, and he had gone with his sisters to say happy birthday to her. When they got to his aunt's house, they met his aunt in the kitchen and they all greeted her. His sisters went in, while he stayed to talk to his auntie, as he was her favourite and loved teasing her.

'I hope you've got some beer in the fridge,' he said cheekily, leaning against the door.

'Beer!' she cried. 'Whatever next?'

'I'm a grown up boy now,' he insisted. 'You don't expect me to drink Coke and Fanta these days do you?'

'Beer, indeed!' exclaimed his aunt. "And what was that I was hearing about girl friends?"

'Don't mind them. I expect my sisters have been gossiping. Did they tell you how scared they are of my fast driving? Auntie Bosun, I wonder who is sixteen today, Kemi or you? You are looking, what's the word, hmn-cute!'

is. There were his cousins, Kemi and Bola, his two sisters, Shade and Yemisi, and two other girls he did not know. He wondered where his aunt's two sons, Olu and Deji, were.

'Hello, girls,' he said brightly. 'Happy birthday, Kemi.' Hmn, Tayo the Great! How are you?' Bola, who was the tomboy of the family, greeted him.

Tayo gave her a mock severe look and shook his head. 'One day, I'll punch your jaw, Bola. What do you call me that for? Stop it, not in front of these pretty chicks! I don't like it, O!'

They all laughed, and he asked where Olu and Deji were, and was told they had gone to buy a present for Kemi, because they forgot to do so the day before.

'And you, where's my present?' Kemi asked him.

'Don't worry. I've got it right here in my pocket,' he said. He fished a little package out of his pocket and gave it to her.

'Hey, thank you, Tayo,' Kemi greeted him.

'Open it and let's see, Kemi. Sly fox, he didn't even tell us he had a present for you,' his sister Yemisi said.

'Don't open it jare, Kemi, until later,' Tayo told her, giving Yemisi a stern look. They all looked inquiringly at him and he shook his head, so Kemi had kept it on the table by her side.

"You haven't introduced your friends to me,' Tayo said. 'Anyway, I'll introduce myself. I'm her big brother, Tayo Browne.'

'Mosunmola Apara,' one of the girls introduced herself, with a smile.

The other girl was smiling too, but said nothing so he looked inquiringly at her.

'Don't tell me you don't know who that is, Tayo,' Shade said, unbelievingly.

'I don't. Do you know me?' he asked the pretty, smiling girl.

"I know you very well, Tayo,' she nodded.

'Well? I'm sorry but I can't place you. Can somebody please help me?' he laughed.

'Blockhead! I'll help you. That's Tope Dina,' Bola said laughing:

"Tope Dina?' Tayo asked blankly.

Yes, silly Billy! Tope Dina from Montgomery Road,' Yemisi confirmed.

stared unbelievingly at the beautiful heart-shaped, smiling face of the young girl. He sat down abruptly on a chair.

You don't mean that dingle-dangle scarecrow Tope, the

skinny girl?'

They all laughed. That had been his nick-name for Tope between him, his cousins and his sisters behind her back, when they were kids.

"That's rude,' said Shade, still laughing.

I'm sorry, but you can't blame me. The thorny bud has really blossomed into a lovely rose. What a beauty she has grown into!

What a transformation! I would never have recognised her, you know. You girls are just incredible. In a couple of years now, she'll be a mother,' he had said, astonished.

They had all laughed and called him a rude boy, but how true his words had turned out to be.

He had found time to talk to her later that day and she told him she was in form five at Our Lady of Apostles Secondary School.

He was in the lower sixth form at King's College, and they talked about the old days at Montgomery Road. He had not been interested in her very much, at the time, because he was almost going steady with Flora Dadzie, his girlfriend at Queen's College. But he was fascinated by the change in Tope. She was not fat but she could not be called skinny either. She was slim but had filled out in all the right places. He asked her if she was still as sickly as before and she said no. Now, she was only sick occasionally. She was suffering from sickle cell anemia, and now that she was almost past her adolescent years, the attacks were less serious and far between. Somehow, they had gone to see a film two days later, and after that, he started two-timing. He saw both Flora and Tope on alternate days, then Flora had got to know about it and had broken up with him. A friend of hers saw them together and told her about it.

He had not minded much and it was only then that he realised he liked Tope better. She dressed elegantly and her makeup which she never did without except when in school uniform was always flawless. He became a regular visitor at Montgomery Road again. By this time she had left school and was working as a clerical officer at the Ministry of Establishments. Then he finished his Higher School too, and got a scholarship to go abroad the next year, to study Electrical Engineering. They were both very much in love by this time.

Everybody, especially auntie Bosun, kept asking him if he knew what he was doing. They drummed it into his ears that Tope was a sickler. It was likely some of their children, if not all, when they eventually got married, would be sicklers too. He was taking on a lifetime's burden of worry and health problems. But he would not listen to anything, and anyway, they were not talking of marriage yet. Most of the time, like Ezinma in Chinua Achebe's Things Fall Apart, Tope would be bubbling with health like fresh palm wine. At other times, which were really very few, she would be very down.

Tayo started working too because he had to wait some time before his school abroad opened. He and Tope talked about getting married when he came back. Then things took a new turn.

Tope became pregnant and she did not tell a soul until she was two months gone. She told Tayo then and he saw red. He raved and shouted at her for the first time in their relationship. Didn't she know the sort of health she had? Didn't she know that, as soon as such a thing happened, she had to go and see her doctor? And anyway, she was supposed to be on contraceptive pills, so how did this happen? Now everybody would blame him. Tope said nothing.

And when they told her parents, her mother started crying. She was sure it would be very unhealthy for Tope to have a baby so young. It was a widespread belief, although it had no medical backing, that sicklers had to be over twenty-one, before it would be safe for them to have babies, as they would have been over the worst of their attacks by then. Oh, what sort of trouble were Tope and Tayo between them bringing on her? She said maybe they could get an abortion on health grounds but Tope would not hear of it. The very next day, she took Tope to the doctor, who examined her and said a D and C was still possible at this stage, but Tope cried and cried and pleaded until they left her with her pregnancy.

Then Tope and Tayo had to get married. It was a very quiet wedding at the Registry and Tope started living with him in his room, in his parents' house. The doctor advised her to stop working and, surprisingly enough, she was in the best of health throughout her pregnancy.

Joy was born and they had all adored her. The birth was easier than they had all expected, even though Tope had had to go into hospital a month before the baby was actually born. She had been very healthy, and had been able to cope with and look after her baby herself quite early. Then it was time for Tayo to go to his school in London. He went alone, and a few months later, Tope and Joy joined him. They had been very happy in their little flat in Battersea. Tope worked as a receptionist in a drug manufacturing company while he went to school, and with her wages and his grant, they had been quite comfortable.

Joy grew up into a lovable little tomboy, and every weekend, they brought her home from her foster parents in Dartford to spend the weekend with them. They made many friends and went out a lot. They were so very happy, and Tope weathered all the five winters she spent in England well. She only had the flu a few times, and then they came back home.

They settled down and life continued pretty much the same. Joy and both her parents remained very close. They spent as much time as they could with her, especially Tope who played ball and all sorts of games with her. She taught her lots of nursery rhymes and songs, and they were more like sisters. They all thought Tope was over the worst, and luckily for them, Joy was the healthiest of children. Tests in England showed that she had no trace of sickle cell anemia in her.

Then when Joy was almost six, Tope became pregnant again, and this time, it was a nightmare. She was nearly always sick, and the doctor said she had to go to the hospital. The doctor told Tayo and their parents that she had not got much longer to live. He said she had leukemia and would not live for more than six more months; he was not even sure if she would last the whole of six months. At this time she was about four months gone, and somehow, she had known that she would not live to look after her baby herself. She accepted the fact that she would not live long and made the most of the little time she had. So she was in hospital, her health deteriorating with every passing day as the months went by, until the baby was born, She had remained cheerful all through her ordeal and the agony she endured.

Enitan's birth, like Joy's, had been fairly easy but Tope lost a lot of blood, and died in her sleep two days later. Though Tope had accepted fate's verdict gracefully, Tayo had felt it badly and thought he would never get over it. At first, he had not wanted to see the baby because, to his bereaved mind, she had robbed him of someone very dear. The love of his life had died giving life to this baby. Then after a couple of weeks, he had been made to realise by his mother that Tope's sacrifice was worth nothing if he did not love Enitan. So he had grown to love her and because she looked like him, and was lovable, he found it easy.

She was christened Amanda (lovable one) Enitan Browne.

His life with Tope had been very very happy, and for a long time after her death, he'd wanted nobody else. He had been content to dwell and fantasize in his memories of the good times they had both had together.

After some time however, he started going out with other women, but he always knew, as soon as he saw them, that he could not love them. So he had given all his love to his daughters, and his time to his work because that was what brought him the money to have a good time. He had been quite content and happy with his life as a playboy until he met Kofo. Why Joy had to go and spoil it all, he did not know. He would teach her a lesson for denying him this second grasp at happiness, he muttered angrily to himself. But oh no, that would be doing exactly what Joy feared would happen. It would confirm all her fears. No, he would have to tread softly. This was slippery ground.

The next day, Joy came to tell him that she would like to work until her results came out.

Why do you want to work, Joy? I thought you wanted to go to Higher School or University this year,' he asked her, looking her straight in the eye.

I want to, but I don't want to stay at home every blessed day, until the results are out,' Joy replied, not meeting his eyes.

Tayo smiled wryly. He could read what was in her mind.

I see. Well, if it's because of Kofo, my dear Joy, you needn't bother. If it's any comfort to you, Kofo has broken off with me.

She won't be around to get in your way,' he told his daughter curtly, reprovingly, as if he blamed her for the split.

Joy looked up sharply and looked down at her toes again.

I'm sorry, daddy, but I can't help how I feel,' she said quietly.

'You can, if you really care to, Joy!' her father retorted, his eyes cold with anger. 'I love Kofo now. I loved your mummy, but you can't love a memory forever. Your mum is no more. Kofo is here.

She can't remove the memory of your mum and she doesn't try to. I don't know how to explain to you. I won't love you less because of her and she loves you too. If you care to know her, you'll know that she is a very nice and warm person. She wants to make me happy and I want to make her happy too, because she's been through a lot of sorrow in her life. But why am I telling you all these things? Never mind, there's no need for all these now. As they say, no use crying over spilt milk,' Tayo Browne told his daughter, with a sigh. 'It's all over.' Joy started crying. 'I'm sorry, daddy. Please forgive me.' He patted her on the head, and went into his bedroom.

Chapter 11

'Mummy, are we not going to live in Enitan's house again?' Bode asked his mother for the umpteenth time.

She shook her head. 'No, Bode, we are not.' 'Not ever?' the little boy persisted.

'No,' Kofo told him and went on cutting the pastries she was making.

'Does that mean Enitan's daddy is not going to be my daddy anymore?' Bode asked again, nearly in tears.

Kofo nodded, the tears stinging at her eyelids too.

'But why, mummy? Did he annoy you?' the little boy persisted fervently.

'Why don't you go and take an ice cream from the fridge, Bode, and let me finish these pastries? Then we will go to grandma's place and you can stay for as long as you like,' Kofo said brightly, trying to change the subject.

'I don't want to go to grandma's place. I want to go to see Enitan and Joy and their daddy,' Bode cried.

'Do as you are told, Bode,' Kofo said sternly.

Bode went crying out of the room.

Kofo felt so bad and sorry. She wanted to call him back, and pet him, but she could not. For the past six weeks, since her break-up with Tayo and her refusal to see him, life with Bode had been so difficult. The little boy was forever asking for Enitan, and her daddy, and wanted to know why they could not all stay together anymore. Kofo did not know what to tell him so he could understand the situation. There was always nothing but tears and scenes in this little flat these days. The lively thing but tears and scenes in this little flat these days. The lively, little chatterbox was gone, and in his place was this sullen, difficult and tearful little boy.

Kofo could not reach him anymore, and he was only happy when he was with his grandparents.

Life now was pretty hectic. Kofo herself missed Tayo and Enitan's liveliness more than anything. She began feeling again the loneliness and ache she used to feel in her heart, when Bobo had first died. Now she understood the poem *Twice have I loved.*

She had loved twice, and had been allowed to taste happiness, both times for only a short period. Maybe she was not cut out for marriage after all, because she could see no other reason why things never worked out for her.

Her mother was shocked, when she heard that Kofo had broken up with Tayo, and all because of Joy.

'But that is only to be expected, and I warned you about it,' she told her daughter.

I know you did, but I can't go through with it, with her feeling this way about me. I can't,' Kofo said.

'My dear Kofoworola, you are not getting younger, you know. Time waits for no one, and the sooner you get settled down, the better for you. This man has told you himself that his daughter will change. What else do you want? For her to like you as Enitan does, right now? That's not possible. If you were in her place, you'd resent someone taking your mother's place too.' Mummy, I'm not marrying Tayo, with Joy feeling this way about me. That's all I know,' she replied.

Her mother looked at her and shook her head, clapping her hands together to express her surprise. 'I always knew you were a fool, Kofoworola Odu, but I never dreamt you were this foolish,' she scolded her daughter.

Kofo had only laughed, and that had made her mother even more angry with her. 'Idiot, what's so funny?' she asked her.

Nothing, mummy. I'm not marrying him, that's all,' Kofo replied, smiling desperately.

Please yourself, but don't say I did not warn you, her mother said, shrugging her shoulders.

"Don't worry, mummy. I won't come running to you, Kofo said, going out of the room. She wished her father was here. He would have understood how she felt, and would have talked to her mother, to see the whole thing Kofo's way.

'Look here, young lady, don't be so rude. You are walking out on me, while I'm talking to you and for your own good too,' her mother snapped at her.

Kofo came back into the room and stood facing her mother. She had not meant to be rude. She had honestly thought that, with that shrug of the shoulders, she had been dismissed.

Why don't you think of Bode instead of thinking only of yourself, Kofo? The boy needs a father,' her mother had pleaded softly, changing her tactics.

Kofo smiled to herself. Never say die. That should be her mother's nickname, she thought. She had realised that abusing Kofo and talking harshly to her would not do any good, so she had changed to speaking gently, and pleadingly. She put her hands on her mother's shoulders.

'Mummy,' she said, 'I never do anything without thinking of what effect it will have on Bode first. Believe me, mummy, I've thought about it a lot and I know that this unhealthy rivalry between Joy and me will do none of us any good.'

'But, Kofo!' her mother began softly.

'Please, mummy, trust me. I know what I'm doing. It's for the best,' she said, and her mother left her alone to her fate. She knew that it would do no good to pursue the matter further that day.

Thinking about it now, Kofo wondered if she was doing the right thing. Oh, God, what sort of mess have I got myself into now? she thought to herself. She wished she had Bobo's attitude to life, then she would not have given a damn what anybody thought or felt about her. She knew that she was not getting any younger.

She needed nobody to rub it in that, at twenty eight, she would soon be left on the shelf if she did nothing about it, but what could she do? Hers was an even worse case because she was twenty eight and an unmarried mother at that. It was common enough to find unmarried mothers around there, but it was not easy for them to find husbands. As her mother said, 'Time waits for no one.'

How these adages contradict one another. What about the one that says, 'There's always tomorrow' and the one that says 'God's time is the best'? It probably was not time for her yet. That was why she would be having these problems. Maybe as the Yoruba adage says, 'The head that is going to be great will meet a lot of troubles and temptations!' Maybe it would be all right for her some day, that was why all this sorrow was hers now. Some day she would know blissful happiness again.

It was Enitan's tenth birthday, and Kofo decided that she would go and say Happy Birthday or poor Enitan would be very disappointed and sad. She bought a pretty birthday card, printed specially for a ten year old, and a lovely dress, which she wrapped nicely in pink paper and pink ribbons. She wondered if she should go and see Enitan in the evening, or in the morning, so as to avoid meeting Tayo. Her heart cried out to her that it was longing to see Tayo, but her head reasoned that it would be better if she did not see him. Kofo's head ruled her heart. She went around noon, and met only Risi, who informed her that both Joy and Enitan had gone to spend the weekend with their maternal grandparents. Kofo left the present and went home.

That night, Tayo came to thank her for the present. Kofo was surprised to see him looking so sad and drawn. Her heart went out to him, but she was not going to let him see how she felt. She let him in and they stood looking at each other like a couple of strangers, each thinking how much they missed the other.

Kofo found her voice first. 'Won't you sit down?' she said, her heart-beats thumping loudly against her chest.

He shook his head. 'No, I'm on my way to give your present to Enitan. I only came to thank you on her behalf. You needn't have 'What a coincidence. Looks just as if we planned it,' Tayo smiled and moved towards her. He put his arms around her, and drew her to him, hugging her as if he would not let her go ever again. 'I missed you, Kofo,' he whispered.

Kofo did not resist for a moment. She knew how much she'd missed the feel of his arms around her, and reveled in the closeness and warmth of the moment, forgetting everything. She stayed there for a couple of minutes and then sanity took over.

She pushed him away and said, 'No, Tayo, we mustn't!'

'Kofo, aren't you going to change your mind?' Tayo asked her, releasing her. 'Be reasonable!'

"Not while Joy's not pleased,' Kofo replied Stubbornly.

'But you are marrying me, not Joy,' Tayo protested wearily.

with him.

'It's all the same, Tayo. Please try to understand,' Kofo pleaded

'All right. I think I'd better go,' he said. 'Goodnight'

'Goodnight,' Kofo said, opening the door for him. 'And give my love to Enitan—and Joy.'

He nodded and she watched his lean frame go out into the dark night. She closed the door and rested her back on it.

The tears started trickling down her cheeks. You must not cry, Kofo. You mustn't, she told herself, and went on crying.

Two days later, Joy sat in her grandparents' sitting room, with her grandmother, and glanced through the classified advertisements page in the Daily Times She looked closely and carefully at the Obituaries, and In Memoriams. There were only two In Memoriams for her mother. One, the nicest, was from her mother's family and the other, which contained a rather small photograph (in Joy's estimation) and very few words, was made Look, mama,

Look at what daddy did for our mummy.' What's wrong with it?' the old woman asked.

It's so small, and the only words that make sense are "Too dear to be forgotten, to live in the hearts of those you love is not to die.

Rest in peace." ' Joy sobbed.

But those are very good and appropriate words, Joy. What more do you want your father to have written?' her grandmother asked her.

He used to write much more than these. I know why he wrote only these,' Joy said.

"Joy! Your mother died ten years ago today. That's a long, long time ago. That's a long time in the life of a young man like your father. He has done well to remember her at all,' her grannie told her.

I know it's because of Miss Odu, mama. How can he let someone take mommy's place?'

Joy, your dad has tried. He's one of the finest of men. *Time changes yesterday*, my dear Joy. Your dad deserves to be happy.

I'm glad he is getting married again,' the old lady said.

'How can you be, mama, when he was married to your daughter?' Joy was astonished that the old lady should sound and look so genuinely pleased about it.

Joy my dear, always remember that yesterday has gone.

Tomorrow is another day. Your dad was hurt terribly by your mother's death. At the time, he was very young. Now he is grasping at another chance of happiness. Tope would not have wanted him to grieve so much for her. I always tell him that.'

'Mama, I don't like her — the woman daddy wants to marry,'

'Kofo? Why not? She's very nice and she's the sort of woman to make your father happy. He loves her and she loves him in rather

ce, Joy said. know likes her

"Joy, look at it this way. If everyone you know likes her, then she must be very nice. Try to accept her for your dad's sake, Mrs Dina told her young granddaughter. "Your father has not even told me when the wedding is going to be,' she added, and was surprised when Joy burst into tears again.

'Oh, nana, I've done wrong. Because I don't like her, Kofo has refused to marry daddy or to see him again,' she sobbed.

'Oh, so that's why your father looks so drawn. I thought he was very sad, myself too. Only two days ago, I was telling your grandfather that your father looked sad and thin to me,' she said.

'Oh, mama, what am I going to do now?'

"You are going to beg Kofo, Joy, that's what you will do. You will ask her to come back to your father and tell her that you are willing to accept her,' her grandmother advised authoritatively.

That evening, Kofo received very unexpected visitors. She was reading, when she heard a knock on her door, and went to open it. She was surprised to see Joy, Enitan and their maternal grandmother at the door. She knelt down and greeted Mrs. Dina, then she greeted Joy and Enitan and asked them all in. They sat down and while they were drinking Cokes, Mrs Dina started telling her about why they had come.

'First of all, dear, we want to thank you for the present you gave Enitan. Then, Joy wants you to know that she is very sorry for all the trouble she's caused you. For her father's sake, she is willing to accept you. She wants her father to be happy once again,' Mrs Dina said. 'Isn't that right, Joy?'

Kofo looked at Joy and Joy, unsmiling, nodded. Then she lowered her eyes and stared at her toes.

Kofo's face glowed with delight. She knelt down and thanked Mrs Dina for her trouble, then she thanked Joy and hugged Enitan.

As soon as they went home, Kofo took a taxi, and went straight to the Brownes' house. Tayo was out, so she waited patiently for him. She waited for a very long time, and as it was getting late, she got tired, and went into his bedroom to lie down. He came in at around 9.00pm, and found Kofo lying down on his bed.

He looked quizzically at her and said, 'Hello.'

'Hello, Tayo,' Kofo said. 'I've changed my mind and come home.'

Tayo stared at her in surprise, not believing his ears.

Kofo got up and went to him. She put her arms on his neck, and kissed him. 'I've missed you terribly, Tayo,' she told him.

'Oh, Kofo, I've missed you too. I can't tell you how much,' Tayo replied, kissing her all over the face, and holding her tightly as if he would never let her go. I've come home, Tayo. When can we get married?" Kofo asked.

'Any time, as soon as you like, my darling, as soon as you like.'

Chapter 12

Six months later, Kofo was in her bedroom, sorting out some clothes, when Sonate put her head in at the door.

'Hello, auntie Kofo. Can I come in?' she asked, smiling at Kofo.

'Nate! Of course, you can come in. I'm doing nothing special,' Kofo told the girl.

She was pleased to see her. Sonate, Tewiah and their mother had been very nice to her, ever since she married Tayo and moved in here. Now that she was pregnant, Mrs Pedro was just like a mother to her. They always had long chats and whenever Kofo felt like discussing anything with a motherly person, she always popped round to Mrs Pedro's place. She could not very well go to her mother's place all the time.

Both Sonate and Joy were classmates now, doing Higher School at the same school, and their friendship was stronger than ever.

Enitan, too, was in Form One at the same school. Sonate and Joy had both made grade two in their school certificate examination and everybody was pleased with them. Sonate had adopted Kofo as one of her elder sisters, but Joy's attitude to Kofo was just polite. She never said more than the necessary things to her. She said 'Good morning' and 'Welcome' and that was barely all. But she was different with Bode. She liked him and was always very nice to him. The two of them always talked for ages. She bought him things and helped him with his homework, any evening she was at home. Kofo was pleased that, at least, she did not mind Bode. In the evenings, when Tayo was at home, and the whole lot of them-Enitan, Bode, Tayo and Risi sat in the sitting room watching television, Joy always went to her bedroom or the Pedros. She hated to see Kofo and her father holding hands, or sharing jokes and confidences or just looking at each other like love-lost teenagers.

Kofo had found out that all the things Enitan told her about Tayo were all fibs and pranks to get them together. She had scolded Enitan but deep in her heart, she had thanked her for bringing her such happiness. She was especially worried about Joy now because she was out most evenings these days. She went out with that good for nothing Tunde Euba. Kofo knew Tunde Euba very well, and knew that he was the love 'em and leave 'em' type. He had befriended a fellow teacher's daughter at Holy Child Nursery, and had left the poor girl high and dry, when he had gotten her pregnant. The teacher, to avoid any embarrassment, had her get rid of the pregnancy before it was showing, and the poor girl had nearly died.

Kofo wanted to talk to Joy about him, but the relationship between them did not allow for such confidential, intimate and heart to heart talks. She had tried all her best to get through to Joy, but it takes two to reach a compromise. Joy was often rude to her and she avoided her as if Kofo was the plague itself.

Her mother had told her, 'You can't win them all,' and she agreed with her. But if she was going to have a successful marriage, Joy was the best ally she could have. For Tayo's sake, she really wanted to be friends with Joy, especially now that she was going to bring an addition to the family.

She wished fervently that Joy would go out with somebody decent, somebody like Tewiah for instance, who really, Kofo could tell, was in love with her. She observed that Tewiah only talked flippantly with Joy, because he knew that her heart was somebody else's. And Joy really could be trying. She never helped at home, but Kofo did not mind as both Risi and Enitan made up for that. Risi was very good, hard-working, cool-headed, tactful, polite and ever-cheerful. She was like a member of the family, and could never do enough for one, and she got on with Kofo like a house on fire.

'These are very lovely dresses, auntie Kofo,' Sonate broke into Kofo's jumbled thoughts.

'Oh, yes. I bought them a few years ago,' Kofo told her, spreading them out for her to see.

'But they are so new and I've never seen you wear them'

Sonate looked puzzled.

Kofo smiled. These were dresses she used to wear when Bobo was alive and he liked her in them. She had refused to wear most of the dresses that reminded her too much of him after his death.

But she kept them, because memories are made of these. Now she could only smile, when she remembered how much happiness these dresses used to bring her, and she looked back on those days without any bitterness. She had tried them on, soon after meeting Tayo and had found that they were a bit tight for her. She wondered if she should give them out to people who really needed them.

'Why haven't I ever seen you wear them, Auntie Kofo?' Sonate asked again. 'They are classicals, you know, the sort of dresses that stay in vogue always.'

'Am I not past all that now?' Kofo teased her, indicating the bulge in her stomach.

'Before that?' Sonate persisted.

'Well, I'm supposed to be a respectable married woman, you know,' Kofo laughed. 'Do you want my husband to chuck me out?'

'Hum, auntie, you are just pulling my leg. You know Joy's daddy would love you in these dresses. You always dress smartly, that's why Tewiah likes you. You know, he told me that if you were not married to Joy's daddy, he would have tried to woo you,' Sonate said, with a twinkle in her eyes.

Kofo thought it was very funny. Tell Tewiah I'm old enough to be his mother, but if he doesn't mind my age. I'll willingly go across the world with him, she joked

'Of course, you are not. Our sisters, Tete and Zinwe, are the same age as you. They'll be twenty eight soon and our brother, Vojo, is only three years younger.'

Kofo laughed again and held out another dress for Sonate to see.

Sonate whooped with delight at the sight of such a pretty dress.

'Gosh, auntie Kofo, why don't you ever wear them?' she gasped.

'Actually, they don't fit me any more,' Kofo told her and added. 'Do you mind if I give you a couple of them? I haven't worn them more than twice,' her eyes pleading with Sonate to accept the offer.

Sonate was filled with joy. 'Mind? Of course I don't. Oh, Auntie Kofo, will you really give me two?' she asked delightedly.

Kofo nodded and asked her to choose two dresses. Sonate wasted no time in choosing the two she liked best. She tried them on and they were just perfect.

'Oh, auntie Kofo, thank you. I just can't resist dresses, you know,' she thanked Kofo gratefully.

'It's nothing, Sonate, my pleasure,' Kofo said. 'Do you think Joy would like some too?' she asked Sonate uncertainly.

'Of course, she won't mind,' Sonate said, without doubt and without thinking. 'I'll help her choose.'

She chose two other dresses and ran out to show all four dresses to Joy. Joy was in the bedroom, when Sonate rushed in, beaming from ear to ear, her arms filled with lovely dresses. Joy was surprised.

Nate! Where did you get all these dresses from?' she asked her.

Just look at them before asking questions, Joy. Aren't they lovely?' Sonate said breathlessly, spreading them on the bed for Joy to see.

'They are,' agreed Joy. 'Are they from sister Zinwe?'

Joy was sure they would be. Sonate's sister, Zinwe, had a good eye for fashion, a better sense of fashion than her twin, Tete, and she was always very generous to Sonate. Joy had always felt that Sonate was the luckiest girl in the world to have such a beautiful and nice sister, but this was the first time she had known her to give Sonate four such lovely dresses, all on the same day. Sonate shook her head.

'Sister Zinwe ke? Give anyone all these lovely new dresses on the same day? You must be joking,' said Sonate, echoing Joy's own thoughts. 'These two are for you, Joy and these two are mine,' she added, handing over Joy's two.

'Oh what a lucky, lucky day for us, Nate, but who are they from? You haven't told me yet,' Joy said, grinning as wide as her mouth would allow.

*Ye, I forgot. They are from auntie Kofo,' Sonate informed her.

The smile left Joy's face as fast as lightning.

'Which auntie Kofo?' she demanded in a whisper.

'How many auntie Kofos do you know?' Sonate snapped at her.

'I'm talking about your stepmother.'

'Hum, Nate, don't call her that.'

"What should I call her? After all she is your stepmother, whether you like it or not,' Nate said irritably.

She was beginning to get very impatient and fed up with Joy's attitude to Kofo. 'My dad's wife, yes, but not my stepmother, because I don't want a stepmother,' Joy said. 'Anyway, whatever you like to call her, she gave you these two dresses,' her friend informed her tartly.

"I don't want them,' Joy said proudly.

'You don't want them?' Sonate asked her in surprise.

'I don't!' Joy repeated.

'So what are you going to do?"

"You will have to take them back to her,' Joy said stubbornly.

'Who? Me? Take them back to her? You must be joking. Not on your life, my friend. If you want to return them to her, by all means, do so yourself. I wonder how you can be so heartless.'

Sonate looked at Joy, as if she could not believe her ears. This was incredible.

"What do you mean by heartless? Don't worry. I'll return them myself,' Joy told her adamantly.

Why do you hate her so much? Let me tell you something, my dear friend, it doesn't do to hate someone. It's the one who hates that suffers. It doesn't touch the one that is hated,' Sonate warned.

I said don't worry.

Let me finish. Auntie Kofo loves you but you won't give her any chance to show how much she cares. You are making her married life a misery, and you know that she deserves so much to be happy. You should have seen the pleasure with which she gave us these dresses. Now you want to hurt her, and make her sad by returning them. I wonder who gave you that name, Joy. It just is not you. Kill-Joy suits you better, my dear friend,' Sonate said angrily.

Joy was angry too. She did not like the way Sonate was talking to her and she blew her top too.

'Please don't lecture me. It's no business of yours how I feel about anybody,' she said. 'Yes, it's no business of mine,' Sonate retorted fiercely. 'I thought I knew you but I realise now, I don't. You are so heartless, so selfish and cruel, always reasoning your own way and giving nobody but yourself any joy. You are making life miserable for your father, your sister and everyone in this house. You are just a selfish girl and as I said before, your name should be Kill-Joy!'

"Well, if that's how you feel about me, I think you'd better go,'

Joy said angrily.

'Yes,' replied Sonate harshly, picking up her two dresses. 'I think I'd better. I'm not sure that I want to be friends with a girl like you any more.'

They had not realised until they both saw Kofo in the doorway that they had unintentionally raised their voices, and the whole argument had turned into a big row. It was their first big quarrel.

Sonate, when she turned round, felt like bursting into tears at the hurt expression on Kofo's face. She brushed past Kofo, mumbled, 'Sorry' and rushed out. Kofo called after her, but she did not even look back. Kofo looked inquiringly at Joy who was looking at her, wondering how much of the argument she had really heard.

Joy picked up the two dresses and held them out to Kofo. I'm sorry. I don't want them,' she said.

Kofo felt as if she'd been dealt a heavy blow. She took the dresses from Joy and walked silently out of the room. She did not know what to say or do. She felt so hurt, so embarrassed and confused that she just burst into tears when she got to her bedroom.

Joy, on her part, was sorry that she had refused Kofo's offer, but she wanted no favours from her. She did not want to ever feel indebted to Kofo. And she saw no reason anyway, why Sonate should take the matter so much to heart. She felt like venting all her anger on Kofo who had caused this row between her and her best friend. She was not going to beg Sonate. How dare she call her Kill-Joy and cruel and selfish and heartless? Those were very harsh and unforgivable things to say to anyone. She expected Kofo to tell her daddy all about what happened that day, but her father came home, the day passed and he said nothing about it, much to Joy's surprise. Her friend Toun's stepmother would have reported such a thing and would have made sure Toun's daddy beat her, had Toun done such a thing.

Two days later, she came home from her date with Tunde to find Enitan watching the late night movie on the telly, alone in the sitting room.

'What are you still doing awake at this time, Enitan?' she asked her little sister, surprised because the latter had always been an early bird.

I was waiting for you, sister Joy, the little girl replied, with a tired yawn.

Why?' Joy asked, puzzled.

"Sister Joy, daddy was saying you go out too much and that he was going to stop you. Then he asked mummy what you do when you come home from school, Enitan said, switching the telly off.

And what did she say?' Joy wanted to know.

"She told him that you always help in the kitchen, except when you have lots of homework and that he should not stop you because you are only enjoying your youth. I think she said you are only young once or something. Then she said you really don't go out much, that most times you are in Sister Sonate's house, reading together,' Enitan told her.

Joy could not believe her ears. This Kofo could always make her feel bad in other people's opinions. Yet ever since she came to this house, she had never once reported Joy to her daddy, and there had been lots of opportunities for her to do so. There had been quite a number of times when Joy was actually rude to her, but they never got to her father's ears. As for being disobedient, that was an everyday occurrence. Kofo only had to give some sort of order and once Joy heard about it, she would disobey her, and flaunt her disregard for Kofo in front of the others. But still Kofo covered up for her. Most times, she spread her clothes out on the line to dry and forgot to take them in. Kofo would take them in for her, but she had never once touched or brought in any of Kofo's washing.

That night, she could not sleep. She kept thinking of all the little things Kofo had done for her since she became their daddy's wife, and came to live in this house. She also thought about what Sonate had said. Kill-Joy she had called her, and she had said Joy was cruel, selfish and heartless. Thinking back on all the unpleasant things she had said and done to Kofo and how nice Kofo had been to her and her friends, whenever she brought them home despite all these, she decided that maybe she was Kill-Joy after all.

'But all Kofo has been doing could be a camouflage, to gain more people on her side, just as she's got Sonate,' a part of her mind argued.

No,' the other half reasoned, 'one could not doubt Kofo's sincerity. She was as plain as A.B.C and never pretended.' Even Joy could give her that. If only she had not quarreled with Sonate, maybe she would have known what to do. She decided that, as from now, she would try to be nice to Kofo. For starters, she would take back those two dresses she refused. But her pride would not let her eat humble pie yet and ask Kofo for the dresses again.

The next day, she came home from school and found that some clothes she had soaked the night before had been washed and ironed. She was so pleased because she had thought about how she was going to manage washing and ironing those clothes with the load of homework they'd been given at school. She ran to Risi to thank her and was told that Kofo was the one behind it. Joy felt very ashamed of herself again but managed to say a polite but cool thank you to Kofo.

That night she stayed in the sitting room to watch telly with Risi, Enitan, Bode, Kofo and her daddy. They were all puzzled by the play that was on. It happened to be one Joy had seen before on stage, so she found herself playing the role of interpreter. She explained to them and somehow found herself talking to Kofo like a friend.

The next day, she summoned up enough will-power to ask Kofo for the dresses. Kofo was surprised, but brought the two dresses out and gave them to Joy without a word. Joy thanked her and went out. The very next day, she wore one of them out for her date with Tunde. The dress fitted her perfectly, like the others fitted Sonate. She had seen Sonate around in both of those dresses but did not speak to her. Joy could not help admiring herself in the mirror, even though she was not feeling particularly happy.

She had realised only that morning that her periods were two weeks overdue, 'Oh, God,' she prayed, 'don't let me be pregnant or my daddy will kill me. She was sure that Tunde would know what to do.

Joy got the biggest shock of her life when she told him. She had been suspecting that he was getting bored with her, but she would not accept or believe it.

You are crazy. What do you mean by saying you suspect you are pregnant?' he had shouted at her when she told him.

I really think I am,' Joy explained as calmly as she could.

"You'd better think well. I never knew you were this stupid. A big girl like you to go and get yourself pregnant!'

'It takes two, you know,' Joy had shouted back at him. 'I wouldn't have been in this position but for you.'

"You could have told me you were too naive to know what other girls of your age do in similar situations,' Tunde said cruelly.

"What do you want me to do? Get rid of it?' Joy asked in a low whisper.

I don't care what you do about it, my dear. Just don't mention my name in connection with it, that's all.'

But you know you are responsible for it. You know you are, Tunde, Joy had cried.

How do I know I'm the only one? I am not getting involved in such things. I have just got a place in the University of Lagos as you well know, and if my father hears of this he won't pay my fees,' Tunde declared.

"So what do I do?' Joy asked plaintively.

'Haven't I made it clear enough? I don't care what you do. Just don't involve me. I am going to be rather busy now. I'd been thinking long before you dropped your news that we should stop seeing each other?'

'And is this the right time for you to tell me that?' Joy asked.

"What better time? I'm sure you'll be able to find your way home. Goodbye and good luck!' he said and walked out on her.

Joy watched him go with her eyes full of tears. He had not even bothered to see her home. He did not have a car but in the past, he had always gone on the bus with her or borrowed his mum's car to take her out. She cried as if her heart would break, especially because she was frightened, and did not know what she would do if she really was pregnant.

The next day, she started crying again. Enitan asked her again and again what the matter was, but she would say nothing, so the little girl went to call Kofo. It was a Saturday, and their father had gone out to play tennis. Kofo was surprised to see Joy crying so heart broken. Joy was a tough nut and she had never seen her cry until today. She sent Enitan and Bode out of the room.

Joy, what's wrong with you?' she asked, alarmed.

Joy did not reply.

"Shall I go and call Sonate?' Kofo asked Joy. Again Joy shook her head.

Sonate and Joy had been quarreling for almost two weeks now and they had both refused all attempts made by elders to settle the quarrel,

'Oh, auntie Kofo! I think I'm pregnant and Tunde has finished with me,' Joy sobbed to Kofo in a whisper.

Kofo's heart lifted and sank almost immediately. She experienced a single moment of happiness when Joy called her auntie Kofo. It was the first time Joy had ever called her that, and she was happy, but here was a serious problem.

"Don't cry any more, Joy,' she said, sitting down by the bed and putting her arms around Joy. 'I'm sorry. Are you crying for Tunde Euba or because you think you are pregnant?'

'Auntie, I'm crying because I'm frightened,' Joy told her.

I'm glad, because he's not worth it. He did the same thing to a girl I used to know. Anyway, don't cry any more. You are not pregnant. How long are you overdue?' Kofo asked her young stepdaughter.

"Two weeks,' came the whispered reply.

'You are not pregnant,' Kofo repeated.

'Because I can tell as soon as a woman is pregnant, and I know Then how come you did not know when you were pregnant with Bode,' Joy demanded.

Kofo smiled wryly. It was such a good question. She did not blame Joy for asking it. She had been both physically and mentally so dulled at the time of Bobo's death that she had not been able to think of herself, let alone know that she was pregnant. She had gone into a corner, like a dog with a hurt, until she had to come out and face things again.

'At first when I was pregnant with Bode, I didn't know. I was too eaten up with grief to bother about what was happening inside me anyway, but I really didn't know.

But Joy, I've seen so many pregnant women, from the early stages of their pregnancies, that I now know the signs. I knew I was pregnant this time as soon as I became a few days overdue.

It's still early yet, but I am quite sure you are not pregnant. So stop worrying,' Kofo explained to her and got up to go.

Joy was so grateful to her. She had desperately needed someone to talk to. She had not expected Tunde to say he would marry her or anything like that, but she had not expected him to be so callous either. Oh, God, how could she have been so cruel to such a nice person as auntie Kofo? she asked herself. Never mind, she would make it up to her for it.

Every day after that, Kofo kept asking her if she had realised her mistake. A week later, she had good news for Kofo, who by this time had become her friend. She had only been overdue. She was so glad that, when she got to school, she said hello to Sonate, and they became friends once more, to everyone's delight. She told Sonate all that had happened and Sonate was really pleased that Kofo and Joy were on the road to friendship. She was wise beyond her years. She didn't say, 'I told you so,' even though she thought it.

A few evenings later, Sonate came to their house and met the whole of the Browne family in their sitting room. They were all watching television. Kofo looked at Joy's happy face and smiled.

How resilient youth is, she thought. Joy was lucky Tewiah was around to help her pick the pieces of her broken heart. Kofo was sure things were going to stay all right for herself and Joy because Joy, who was a partygoer, had refused to go to one with Tewiah on Saturday. In her own words, she wanted to spend the day with her family because it was her stepmother's birthday. Kofo cherished those words and wished she could set them to music.

Bode, who was a chatter-box, was unusually quiet today.

"What's wrong with you, Bode?' Joy asked him, tickling his tummy.

Bode did not laugh, much to everyone's surprise. He loved being tickled and everybody knew that.

'Charlie said that daddy's going to like the baby better than me, because he is not my real daddy, and he is the baby's real daddy,' Bode said sullenly.

Everybody stared at him. The baby was not yet here and it was causing such a controversy. Charlie was their neighbor's son and he was the same age as Enitan. He was a very rough and unruly boy, but he loved playing with Bode.

'Hum, Charlie is a liar. Tell him I said so!' Enitan exclaimed.

'Yes, tell him I said so too. Of course daddy loves you, as much as he loves Enitan and me. He doesn't even know the baby yet, so how can he love the baby more than you?' Joy added quickly.

'What if he is a boy?' Bode asked.

'Boy or girl, it doesn't matter, Bode. Daddy will still love you very much. You are the first boy in this family, so you stand a better chance, if you are a good boy,' Joy explained to him, patiently.

'Yes, that's true. You are special because you are our first son, just as Joy is our first daughter, Bode,' Tayo Browne added for good measure, lifting Bode up onto his knees.

Kofoworola Browne looked gratefully at Joy, smiled weakly and winced with pain, as the baby kicked hard. 'Now, we are a real family. So, hurry up and come, baby,' she said wordlessly.

Milton Keynes UK
Ingram Content Group UK Ltd.
UKHW021013291124
451807UK00015B/1223